MOON OF MADNESS

MOON OF MADNESS

SAX ROHMER

Originally published in 1926-1927.

Published by Wildside Press.
Visit us online at wildsidepress.com.

CHAPTER I

THE GERMAN LINER

"I SHOULD *LOVE* A long glass of iced German lager," said Nanette. "Besides, I refuse to be deserted for a whole morning."

Her Japanese parasol lay along the rail of the veranda, her round bare elbows rested upon it and she cuddled her obstinate little chin in upturned palms. I turned to her with a glance in which I had meant to convey rebuke. But the blue eyes danced with mischief and pouting lips smiled impudently, a smile half childish and half elfin.

"Young ladies of eighteen do not drink beer," I answered paternally. "It isn't done."

Jack Kelton came out as I spoke, saw Nanette, and flushed like a girl. When I say "like a girl" I mean like a girl of Victorian literature. To-day one should say "like a boy." I never saw Nanette blush during all the time I knew her. I saw her grow deathly pale; but this was later.

Jack was good to see in the Madeira sunlight; one of those lean-limbed young Oxonians who strip so well and who always look amazingly clean. Nanette turned a slim shoulder in his direction, and stared out pensively across the bay. I thought that she had the most perfect arms imaginable. So did Nanette.

"I want to go out with you two and Mr. Ensleigh to that ship," she said, peering aside at the enraptured Jack. "Please ask Mumsy. She likes you—and I love beer."

Jack and I exchanged glances. We both looked at Nanette; and then beyond to where the subject of controversy lay anchored—a big German out of Bremen, in from the River Plate.

"I *have* asked her," Jack declared. "She's adamant."

"So have I," came a cheery voice—and Ensleigh joined the party. "She says that Mr. Kirby is coming to lunch."

"But I *loathe* Mr. Kirby!" cried Nanette, turning upon the speaker scornfully. "He's one of the reasons why I want to go!"

"Is that so, Nan?"

From a long, awning-covered chair near the corner of the veranda Nanette's mother arose—a gracefully pretty woman who solved the mystery of Nanette's beauty for those who had met only her father.

"Mumsy! Have you been sitting there all the time?"

"All the time, dear—and I have heard every word! So don't attempt to take one back!"

Ensleigh, the well-groomed, became all attention. He became attentive from the crown of his perfectly brushed hair to the soles of his spruce white shoes. He placed a chair for Nanette's pretty mother. He focussed his Zeiss glasses to enable her to view the German liner. She thanked him with a smile that was very like Nanette's.

"So you loathe poor Mr. Kirby?" she murmured, raising the glasses.

"Hate him poisonously!"

"And you love beer?"

"Simply worship it, Mum! Lager is my vice!"

Her mother lowered the glasses and fought with rising laughter, for Nanette was looking straight at her. Then:

"You little devil!" she said. "I don't believe a word of it! But your father simply won't hear of you going on board a German ship. Don't ask me why. You know him as well as anybody."

"I'll ask him myself!" Nanette said, flashing blue eyes rebelliously. "Where is the funny old thing?"

"Nan, dear!"

"Oh, he's a darling! But he *is* funny! He's never forgotten that I was once a baby."

"You are still a baby, Nan—a mere infant."

Nanette threw back her shapely bobbed head and laughed scornfully. Wild canaries were love-making in the palm grove below the balcony, and, being poetically inclined, I suppose, I thought that Nanette's soft rippling laughter was music sweet as theirs.

She turned swiftly. She had all her mother's grace as well as the divine abandon of youth. With never another glance at any of us, she walked in through the open French window. Jack Kelton's glance followed the slim, straight figure. Her mother looked up at Ensleigh.

"Have you a daughter?" she asked.

"No," he replied. "I regret——"

"Don't regret," she interrupted; but her smile belied the Chinese solecism to come: "Pray that you may never have a daughter!"

"Really," Jack began, in his youthful, diffident way, "I don't think there's any harm in——"

He was interrupted. Nanette returned, dragging by the hand a very bored, gray-haired gentleman who carried a copy of the *Times* that was ten days old. The gentleman, blinking through his glasses, was being forced out into the sunshine.

"Now, Pop," said Nanette firmly, "is there really any reason why I shouldn't go with Mr. Ensleigh, Mr. Decies, and Mr. Kelton to see that German liner?"

"Well, dear," her father replied, in his laboured manner, "I am afraid you would be late for lunch, and——"

His glance sought his wife's. I distinctly detected a negative shake of the head from Nanette's mother.

"And," he went on, "your mother thinks that this would be rude, as Mr. Kirby is expected."

He smiled almost apologetically, patted Nanette on the head, and, *Times* in hand, returned to his shady lair in the smoke-room. Nanette stared reproachfully at her mother.

"Don't be huffy about it, darling," said the latter. "Really, you will only have time for a swim and a sun bath, if you are to make yourself presentable by one o'clock."

Nanette looked swiftly from face to face. A number of people had now begun to come out from late breakfast. She checked speech, withered poor Jack with a final, comprehensive look of scorn, and walked quickly into the hotel. The last few steps that were visible, as she crossed the threshold, almost consisted of stamping her little feet.

Following a moment of silence:

"Look here, you chaps," said Jack, "it looks rather mean for us all to desert Nanette. I know we've engaged the launch and all that, but it's beastly tame swimming alone——"

"Don't worry, Mr. Kelton," Nanette's mother broke in. She was smiling. "Nanette will not be swimming alone!"

Poor Jack smiled in return, flushed, and then frowned darkly. His glance constantly sought the entrance to the hotel. But Ensleigh tactfully made the conversation general, and we were discussing the feminine modes of Paris as opposed to those of Buenos Aires when a slight figure arrayed in a pink bathrobe and shaded by a Japanese parasol passed slowly down the path below the terrace; whereupon:

"There goes Nanette!" said Jack, jumping up. "Excuse me. I'll just run and ask her if she would rather I stayed."

He hurled himself in the direction of the steps and disappeared. A moment later he reappeared, running after the girl. We watched.

"Nanette!" he called.

Nanette paused, turned, waved her hand, and went on. She walked under a veritable awning of hibiscus, sweeping some of the blossoms off with her parasol. Rounding the corner, she came into view again on a lower path. Her mother leaned over the balcony rail.

"Go after her, Jack!" she called. "Don't be afraid of her!"

The words reached Nanette. She looked up through flower-laden branches. Her voice came faintly.

"I don't want him to come after me. I want to be alone."

Jack Kelton turned and began to walk back up the sloping path. He kept his curly head lowered, taking out a briar from his pocket and fumbling for his pouch. Nanette's mother glanced at Ensleigh.

"Poor Jack," she said. "He is very young!"

CHAPTER II
RESCUE

WE DID NOT TAKE the lift down to the landing-stage. It was busy with bathers; therefore we descended by the rambling stairway cut out of the rock. At the bend, I paused.

Half across the bay, far beyond the waddling group who hugged the bathing pool, where the transparent water showed turquoise blue, I saw a flashing of white limbs and glimpsed a pink-covered head lowered to the swell. Came a rapturous murmur behind me.

"Nanette! Gad! That girl swims like a fish!"

"They should follow with the boat," Ensleigh's voice broke in on Jack's. "There's a beastly current cuts round the headland."

"She is safe enough," said I. "Her fairy godmother was a mermaid—or a siren."

Nevertheless, when we reached the waiting launch, Nanette's daring had attracted attention. I could not see her mother; but there was a buzz of excited conversation all around, and the brown-skinned professional was making urgent signals to the boatmen.

"She's right on our course!" cried Jack. "Come on! Hurry up!"

"Don't worry," I implored him, tumbling into the launch.

"But she'll never be able to swim it!" said Ensleigh, jumping in behind me. "Hullo! What's this!"

He had stumbled over a bulky parcel wrapped up in newspaper. I thought I recognized the *Times*.

"Please leave alone, sir!" cried the Portuguese in charge. "I aska tella you no touch!"

"Oh!"

Ensleigh stared at him suspiciously, and then we were off.

"Pick her up, Decies!" came a shout from someone on shore. "She's overdone it this morning. She can never get back!"

The purr of the motor made it difficult to hear the other shouts that followed us. But excitement was growing intense, and I looked out ahead uneasily. I could not see Nanette.

"Can you see her, Decies?" said Jack hoarsely.

"No."

"There she is!"

The cry came from Ensleigh, and:

"Where?" Jack and I yelled together.

Ignoring us:

"Port, easy!" he directed the man at the wheel. "Now—as she is! Hold it!"

We raced, all out, in the direction of the rash swimmer. A sort of anger claimed me. This crazy performance was a display of girlish pique. I felt particularly sorry for Jack Kelton. He was hanging over the bow in a perfect anguish of terrified expectation. Presently:

"She's still swimming strongly!" he gasped; then, almost immediately: "My God!"

"What?"

Ensleigh and I were peering ahead over Jack's shoulder.

"She's gone down!"

Over the noise of the motor, over the sound of the sea, it reached us dimly—a prolonged, horrified cry from the watchers on shore.

What happened during the next few minutes I am unable to record. I think Jack was fighting with the boatman because he couldn't get another amp. out of his engine. Ensleigh, I remember, looked dishevelled for the first time in my experience of him. I was drenched with perspiration—and it was not wholly due to the heat of the sun.

Then, dead ahead, not six lengths away, a white arm was thrown up out of the sea.

"Stop her!" I yelled.

Hot on the words came a splash—and Jack was in. He was fully dressed, except that he had shed his college jacket. He reached Nanette as she came up for the second time.

"Reverse! Starboard!"

We described an untidy crescent; and then—Nanette was being hauled aboard. She sank down on the cushions as Jack came clambering over looking like a half-drowned Airedale.

"Nanette!" he panted, and dropped on his knees before her.

She opened starry eyes, and looked at him.

"Yes?" she said.

"Back to the landing-stage," I heard Ensleigh direct the boatman.

"What's that!" cried Nanette, surprisingly sitting upright. "Not on your life, Pedro!"

We were riding the swell, the motor silent, and from the now-distant bathing pool I heard a sound of great, prolonged cheering.

Nanette sprang up on the thwart, standing there, poised on tip-toe, a slender young goddess. Jack's coat was in her hand; and she waved it furiously, looking back to where moving figures showed upon flower-draped terraces.

The cheering was renewed.

"That will relieve Mumsy's anxiety," said Nanette, sitting down again. "Please go ahead, Pedro—and would somebody pass me my robe?"

"What!" cried Jack.

Ensleigh tore away the pages of the *Times* from the mysterious bundle—and there was Nanette's pink robe!

"Be careful, please!" she said. "My shoes are wrapped up in it." She turned to Jack, at the same time pulling off her pink bathing cap. "I'm so sorry you jumped in," she added. "You were a darling to do it, though."

He had been positively glowering at her; but, at this, he blushed with delight and became a proud and happy man. Nanette shook her tousled head distractingly. Stooping, she pulled out from the folded robe a pair of high-heeled shoes and proceeded to squeeze five tiny wet toes into each of them.

"Nanette!" I said slowly. "Weren't you drowning?"

She looked up at me.

"Of course I wasn't drowning!" she returned. "I was swimming under water. I was good for another mile!"

"Nanette!" said Ensleigh. "You will come to a bad end, my child."

"Please pass me my parasol," Nanette retorted. "It's in the locker. And be careful. My bag is inside it."

The Japanese parasol was discovered. From it, Nanette took a small bag. Surveying herself disdainfully in a square mirror, she combed her hair. She delicately applied lip salve and powdered her impudent nose.

"You are all wet!" said Jack, feasting his eyes.

His case was worse than hers, and I marvelled at the altruism of love.

"The sun will dry me. But, oh! how good that lager will taste! Won't someone please give me a cigarette?"

I held out a yellow packet, and:

"Nanette," I said, "one day a Someone will come who will teach you how to behave yourself!"

"Tosh!" said Nanette, taking a Gold Flake. "I've outlived that sheikh stuff."

CHAPTER III
THE MAN FROM THE RIVER PLATE

As we drew alongside the German, it became evident that we were objects of much interest to her people. I had a good view of the third-class quarters; she had a deck-load of dagoes under her awnings that would have frightened a Chicago bootlegger.

We started up the ladder; and I thought it probable that some of the spectators would either fall overboard or break their necks, so urgently did they crane across the rails.

"They are anxious to see the gallant rescuer," said Ensleigh.

I knew my dago better. They were anxious to see Nanette's pretty legs.

On the deck, I turned and looked across to where Funchal climbed the hill. The sunlight was dazzling. I could trace the steep cobbled street, from point to point, down which one may slide in a wicker toboggan; see the square, too, with its powder-blue trees, and imagine the morning gathering at the tables outside the Golden Gate. Away over the bows I looked, and saw the flower-draped cliffs below Reid's, where, on the lower terrace, over cocktails, Nanette would, I surmised, be the sole topic of conversation.

The lady in question, supremely indifferent to the somewhat marked curiosity of the passengers, was walking aft with Jack, doubtless in quest of the much-desired lager. Jack, his legs encased in sodden flannels, was ridiculously happy because Nanette hung on his arm.

"Leave them alone," said Ensleigh. "God knows he's earned it."

We found our way to the smoke-room and ordered drinks. They were good and cheap. They served to wipe out one more of the old scores I had against our Teutonic friends (*nées* enemies). It was a distinctly mongrel company. Germans predominated, with a big sprinkling of those nondescripts and none-such usually invoiced as Argentines but sometimes mistaken for Greeks.

One man, who sat alone, puzzled me. He was handsome, in a way. He wore his wavy hair rather long and was dressed in a perfectly cut and immaculately white drill suit. With the aid of a black-rimmed monocle attached to a thick ribbon, he read what looked like an official document.

"By Jove!" Ensleigh exclaimed.

Glancing aside, I saw that he, too, was staring at this romantic individual.

"Looks like John Barrymore," said I.

"I know," Ensleigh replied. "But he didn't wear his hair like that the last time I saw him—coming out of the Salient with what was left of the Irish Guards. By Jove!"

He jumped up and crossed the room. I followed.

"O'Shea!" he cried.

The man addressed dropped his monocle and stood up; then:

"Ensleigh!" he exclaimed, and held out his hand. "Can it be Ensleigh!"

"Ensleigh it is!" was the reply; "and I want you to meet"—drawing me forward—"Mr. Decies. Decies, this is Major Edmond O'Shea."

The Major readjusted his monocle and looked me over briefly, as if to determine whether he wanted to know me or not. I found myself looking into a pair of the coldest gray eyes that had ever examined my hidden motives.

But, to tell the truth, I was more than a little flurried. For, as Ensleigh spoke, the fact had dawned upon me that I stood in the presence not only of an Irishman of ancient family, nor merely in that of a distinguished British officer, but in the presence of a mess-room tradition; a thing infinitely more wonderful and holy. This was "The O'Shea"—a synonym for all that's fine under the Colours from Whitehall to Khatmandu.

He dropped his monocle and grasped my hand warmly.

"I am glad to meet you, Mr. Decies," he said. We formed a trio, and there were some inevitable reminiscences—and more drinks; then:

"What, in the name of wonder, are you doing on this ship?" Ensleigh asked.

O'Shea shrugged his shoulders. He had some queerly Gallic mannerisms. In fact, if one had not known better, one must have written him off as an incurable poseur.

"Peace-time soldiering is a dull business," he replied. "I take on odd jobs to keep me out of mischief."

He rang for the steward and ordered drinks in what I believe was unexceptionable German. Following some aimless chatter:

"Are you for Bremen?" asked Ensleigh.

"I don't know," said O'Shea surprisingly. He twirled his glass and stared around the smoke-room. "I may come ashore here."

"You *may*!" I exclaimed and glanced at the clock. "You have twenty minutes to decide!"

"Two would be sufficient," he assured me. "I travel light!"

He smiled—and, in the smile, I met for the first time the real O'Shea. The cold gray eyes were cold no longer; they smiled, too—whimsically, lovably.

The cloak of inscrutability was dropped, just for a moment, and the clean, brave soul of the man peeped out. A vague dislike vanished as morning mist, and I knew that men would follow Edmond O'Shea into the thickest and the hottest, if he needed them; women, too, perhaps. A man like that is a man born to suffer. But suddenly I understood why the Guards had worshipped him.

"There goes the first shore signal," said Ensleigh. "We had better rescue Nanette from the lager."

We found her on deck with Jack and another man who had tacked himself on to the party. He was a poisonously handsome none-such, and his heavy-lidded dark eyes were literally devouring the girl's dainty beauty. He had come across Jack in London; and now Jack was the most unhappy man in Madeira. Every time roguish blue eyes met lustful brown eyes, he visibly shuddered.

The dark gentleman was presented.

"Ensleigh, Decies—meet Senhor Gabriel da Cunha."

We met him—reluctantly.

"This," said Ensleigh, "is Mr. Jack Kelton—Major Edmond O'Shea. Doubtless, Senhor da Cunha, you have met already?"

"No," murmured O'Shea, bowing coldly. "One does not meet everybody on board."

"Nanette!" I called.

She had stepped to the rail with Da Cunha. She turned.

"Yes?"

"I want you to know Major Edmond O'Shea."

She came forward and I introduced them formally. Nanette gave one quick, startled look at O'Shea—and O'Shea, noting her unusual attire, smiled. Nanette dropped her lashes, said something meaningless, and ran back to Da Cunha.

I heard Jack grind his teeth. When he joined the pair at the rail I stood at his elbow.

"We must be saying good-bye, Mr. da Cunha," he began, but:

"Not good-bye at all!" Da Cunha exclaimed, turning and resting one hand on Nanette's shoulder. "I am undecided until this morning, but now—it is settled! Here, in Madeira"—he indicated distant hills—"I have a bungalow, so charming. Do you know—" he included us all in the conversation—"that in Funchal is what they call a 'blind spot' in radio? Yes. But in my bungalow, high up, I have the most perfect set in the island; and one night—to-night, maybe—" he glanced aside at Nanette—"we shall dance to your Savoy band!"

"You are going ashore, then?"

"But certainly! It is settled. Is it not?"

The question was addressed to Nanette, and:

"I should just *hate* to lose you so soon," she replied. "Let's go and see if your things are in the boat."

Side by side with the radiantly smiling Da Cunha, she hurried forward. She glanced at Jack, at me, at Ensleigh. O'Shea was watching her, but she avoided his gaze. He turned and went in at the saloon entrance.

The last gong sounded. Jack had suddenly disappeared. I stared at Ensleigh. He whistled softly.

"Nanette has been bitten at last," he remarked.

"Yes," I said, "I think she has."

Da Cunha's baggage was loaded into Reid's launch and we all got aboard. We were surrounded by a babbling gang in boats who held up Madeira lace and cane chairs and shawls and bedspreads, desperately inviting bids from the passengers. It was distracting, so that I scarcely noticed a steward coming down the ladder, carrying a suitcase and a valise. Jack sat right astern, his hands plunged in the pockets of his sodden flannels. Then, suddenly, I realized that someone was beside me.

I turned—and met the cold gray eyes of O'Shea!

"Good heavens!" I exclaimed. "Your decision was a sudden one!"

"Yes," he replied, "it was—very."

"Hullo, O'Shea!" cried Ensleigh. "This is fine!"

Nanette bent toward Da Cunha, talking animatedly.

CHAPTER IV
AT THE CASINO

A PARTY OF US went down to the Casino that night, consisting of Nanette, Nanette's mother, Ensleigh, and myself. Jack excused himself on the plea that he had promised to play somebody five-hundred up. Nanette had been put through the hoop well and truly for her escapade, but she looked none the worse for this parental correction.

Newly from the seclusion of a French convent, she was learning the dangerous truism that beauty governs mankind.

Da Cunha was waiting at the Casino—and Nanette pretended to be surprised. Her mother really *was* surprised, and maternally alarmed. She was a woman of the world and she knew her Da Cunhas.

The said Da Cunha wanted to dance. Nanette loved dancing and danced divinely. Therefore she decided to play roulette.

"Please, Mumsy," she pleaded—"until I have lost a pound!"

Her mother consented, silently signalling me to sit beside Nanette at the table. Whilst Nanette's mother danced with Ensleigh, I chaperoned Nanette.

The game was dull. Da Cunha constantly urged the superior charms of the ballroom. But Nanette played on. Presently:

"Do you think Jack will come along?" she asked.

"I hope so."

An interval in which Nanette lost five shillings, then:

"Had you met Major O'—what's his name—before?"

"No. I had heard of him."

"Really? Is he famous?"

"I suppose he is—in a way."

"But listen!" Da Cunha exclaimed, "this is *so* boring! Let us dance."

"Not until I've lost my pound," said Nanette firmly.

More aimless play, then:

"I saw your Major man when we first went on board, you know," said Nanette, casually staking her all on a number. "Jack and I peeped into the smoke-room, and—he was in there."

"Really. Is that so?"

"Yes. Wasn't it odd I should meet him, after—seeing him like that?"

"Very odd."

Nanette's fortune was swept away by the croupier. She remained unperturbed. She kept throwing quick little glances all about the room, and now:

"Please take me out on the terrace and get me a long, cool drink," she asked.

We stood up and crossed to the open doors. Da Cunha grabbed Nanette's arm and led her out. As I followed, I glanced aside, and saw Jack coming in. He looked very flushed. He was literally glaring after the pair in front of me. I waved to him, but he swung around and went out again.

It was dark on the terrace and at first I couldn't see Nanette. Then I glimpsed a raised white arm over in a distant corner. She was standing with her back to the railing and Da Cunha stood in front of her, bending forward, one hand resting beside her and his face very close to hers.

"What about that long, cool drink?" said I.

Nanette immediately ran to me.

"Oh, please!" she cried. "I'm simply gasping! Where shall we sit? Somewhere by the windows—where we can watch."

She was excited, and it was clear enough that Da Cunha had been making love to her. He turned, and I heard him snap his fingers.

"Why not here?" he suggested. "How beautiful is the view in the moonlight, with the dark groves and twinkling lamps."

"No," said Nanette, selecting a table near an open window. "I feel chilly and I want to watch the dancing."

"If you are cold, let us dance."

Nanette shook her head and opened a tiny jewelled cigarette case. She bent toward me.

"A match, please," she begged.

She was quite determined, and so we sat there sipping iced drinks until Nanette's mother and Ensleigh joined us. There were inquiries for Jack, but I said nothing—for the boy had been palpably drunk.

Nanette was unable to mask her preoccupation, constantly looking into the lighted rooms, then, suddenly, halfway through a Charleston, she jumped up.

"Come on," she said to Da Cunha, and threw her wrap to me—"let's dance!"

He was on his feet in an instant and the two went in. Nanette's mother was playing, and as I stood up I glanced toward the table.

O'Shea was standing watching the play.

Nanette and Da Cunha began to dance. Da Cunha danced perfectly, with all the sensuous grace of a none-such; but the look in his dark eyes raised my gorge to a hundred and twenty in the shade. Nanette floated in his arms like a bit of thistledown; her tiny feet seemed scarcely to brush the floor. He talked to her constantly, and sometimes she smiled up at him; but, always, she glanced into the roulette room as they passed. Ensleigh joined us.

"Yes," said he, "little Nanette is in the throes of her first infatuation."

As he spoke, she went past in Da Cunha's arms, and frowned at Ensleigh—because he blocked her view of the roulette table.

"She is," I agreed.

She danced every dance after that with Da Cunha, becoming more and more animated as the night wore on. Then her mother moved an adjournment. Of course, Nanette objected.

"Mumsy," she said. "Mr. Da Cunha has invited us all to drive up to his bungalow. We can dance to the Savoy band. Think of it!"

But her mother refused to think of it. Da Cunha was not defeated yet, however. His car was waiting. He would drive the party to Reid's. In the end this invitation was accepted. Nanette, her mother, Ensleigh, and I elected to go.

"How many can you take?" Nanette asked.

"Oh, six easily."

"I wonder if anyone else is going back?" said Nanette.

Following her glance:

"I might ask Major O'Shea if he is ready," said I. "Do you mind, Senhor da Cunha?"

"But of course not!" he replied, looking like Cæsar Borgia thinking out a new prescription.

O'Shea thanked me. He preferred to walk.

"And I dislike Senhor Da Cunha," he added.

Therefore the five of us packed into a flamingo-red Farman that stood before the Casino. I thought that if brass helmets had been served out, we should have done credit to any fire brigade. Da Cunha, of course, had Nanette beside him in front. I could hear his constant murmur over the roar of the engine. He took us up to Reid's at an average of about fifty-five.

Nanette's mother steered Nanette to bed, and Da Cunha did not stay long. I sent a page to look for Jack, but he was not in his room.

At about midnight, O'Shea joined us. We went out on to the terrace, pipes going, and sat watching the fairyland of the gardens below, with the winking lights of Funchal climbing the slopes beyond. Presently I heard a faint movement, and:

"Oh!" said a voice in the darkness.

We all turned—and there was Nanette, distracting in déshabille.

"I can't sleep, and I left my book out here!" she explained.

"Let me look," said Ensleigh.

But he looked in vain.

"May I stay awhile and smoke a cigarette with you?" Nanette pleaded; "or were you telling funny stories?"

She stayed—seated on the arm of my chair. There was not much conversation, but after awhile O'Shea got up and disappeared. Nanette began to talk, then, with feverish animation, until presently O'Shea came back, carrying a loose coat.

Very gracefully, he placed it around Nanette's shoulders.

"You must be cold," he said.

Nanette glanced up at him, then down again—and shivered. But it was not because she was cold.

Later, long after Nanette reluctantly had retired to her room, Jack was driven up from Funchal. We put him to bed without arousing anyone.

"I'll kill that slimy Da Cunha," he declared thickly—and went to sleep.

O'Shea surveyed him through the black-rimmed monocle.

"I wonder if cats and pretty girls know how cruel they are?" he murmured.

CHAPTER V
"IN FIVE MINUTES"

THE DAYS WORE ON in that lotus-eaters' paradise and I became an audience of one at a comedy designed to end in drama. There was a mystery that intrigued me vastly, and Ensleigh shared my curiosity.

I could not imagine what the O'Shea was doing in Madeira.

Da Cunha, palpably, had broken his journey to pursue Nanette. He positively haunted the hotel. I found it hard to believe that any such motive had inspired the Major. Ensleigh, with singular density, believed that Nanette was desperately infatuated with Da Cunha. I let him think so, and studied O'Shea.

This strange man spent a large part of every day seated on his balcony, reading and writing. What he read or what he wrote, nobody knew. On occasions, he disappeared for hours: and no one knew where he went.

It was queer, too, how many times Nanette strolled through the unfrequented part of the gardens below this balcony. Sometimes, but rarely, she would be alone, sometimes with Jack, more often with Da Cunha. But, always, she paused to glance in her mirror and powder her nose before she turned the corner. O'Shea, apparently, never noticed her.

She would loiter around the bathing pool for hours in the morning and then suddenly throw off her robe and plunge into the sea with an easy, gliding dive like a young dryad. By this token I would know that O'Shea was sauntering down the steps.

As she went in, Da Cunha and Jack would take the water like twin ducks. It was a miracle that they never tried to drown each other.

O'Shea was a hard man to know; a lonely man. I was honestly proud of the fact that, little by little, he began to unbend to me, to grant me something like friendship. Occasionally he would join me on the cocktail terrace before lunch; and Nanette would ask him for matches and then run back to her mother, Ensleigh, Jack, Da Cunha, and the rest of the party who, amongst them, had enough matches to fire the building.

Da Cunha was ceaselessly persevering in his endeavours to take her for drives, to take her fishing, and to dance with her to the strains of the Savoy band. Her mother negatived these plans.

One day a very (apparently) indignant Nanette came across to where I was sitting with O'Shea. Jack followed.

"Mr. Decies!" she burst out, "Gabriel wants to drive me out to a perfectly wonderful cliff. You lie on the edge and look down I don't know how many hundred feet. Now, do *you* see any earthly reason why I shouldn't go?"

"I don't suppose Decies sees any earthly reason why *I* shouldn't," said Jack. "But I haven't been invited."

"You are always quarrelling with Gabriel," Nanette retorted, fixing a cigarette in her holder. "Please, Major, would you give me a light?"

As she stooped over the match that he struck for her, I could see her eyes—looking at every wave in his hair, seeking out the hint of powder at his temples, studying his long, sensitive fingers. He threw the match away, and:

"You are such a restless little girl," he said. "Why not spend a few peaceful hours in the garden, reading? Let me lend you a book."

Coming from any other source, this suggestion would have provoked a scathing rejoinder, but:

"Thank you," said Nanette simply, "I will."

She sat for that entire afternoon in a secluded corner of the garden, a comfortable, empty chair drawn up beside her own, reading a Russian novel—and waiting for O'Shea to join her.

But he didn't.

That evening the comedy became drama. I was to learn in a few short hours how Nanette's alluring beauty had averted tragedy from a royal house. And this was how it developed:

A rather special dance had been arranged—I forget why; and O'Shea, quite the best-dressed man in the hotel, was last to go to his room and first down. He could get into black quicker than anyone I have ever met. You may know Reid's green and yellow jazz cocktail bar? Well, as I looked in, having changed, there was O'Shea on a tall stool studying a dry Martini through his monocle. The way his bow was tied excited my envy; it was a poem in white piqué.

We had the bar to ourselves, and presently: "How long do you expect to stay in Madeira?" I asked.

He shrugged his shoulders and smiled—that rare and revealing smile.

"In the strictest confidence, Decies," he replied—and suddenly his gray eyes grew steely; he was smiling no longer—"until I have in my possession a certain small black dispatch-box."

"What!" I exclaimed.

"It contains," he went on, "some unfortunate correspondence compromising a royal personage; and if it ever reaches the Communist base in London, I hesitate to imagine the consequences."

"Good heavens!" said I, and formed my lips to convey an unspoken name. O'Shea nodded.

"Exactly," he replied. "That was what took me to the Argentine; but the Reds' man—a dangerous and clever agent—doubled on me in Buenos Aires, and so you met me on my way back to Europe."

"Then you have it!" I cried.

"No, damn it! I haven't!" said he; "or would I be sitting on this stool? It's getting desperate, Decies! There's a British destroyer standing off Funchal waiting my radio that I'm coming on board!"

I said nothing for a few moments. Then I thanked him for his confidence.

"I confide in you with a definite purpose," he replied. "I claim to be a judge of men, and I judge you to be one who would stand by in a rough house. I may need help, after all. If I do, the facts being as we know them, can I call on you?"

We solemnly shook hands—as Nanette came racing in.

She was flushed with excitement, and wearing a new frock. Her blue eyes shone like stars when she saw O'Shea. She looked adorable, and was well aware of the fact. Her happiness was that of the girl who knows herself to be perfectly gowned. It was completed now that Fate had ordained O'Shea to be the first man to see her so.

Jumping on to a tall stool:

"Do you like me?" she demanded naïvely.

"You look as though you had come straight from fairyland," I said. "Let me order you something, to prove you are mortal."

"Oh, no, please!" cried Nanette. "Mumsy would play Hamlet if she caught me drinking cocktails! Give me just a sip of yours!"

She drank from my glass, watching me with roguish eyes; then, turning to O'Shea:

"Am I smart enough to be honoured with a dance this evening, Major?" she asked—but the note of raillery faded as she met his glance, and she dropped her bobbed head, looking down at tiny blue and silver shoes.

"The honour would be mine, Nanette," he said, in the gentle way he had of addressing all women.

Nanette bit her lip and jumped to the floor, as her mother came to look for her.

"Good gracious, Nanette!" she exclaimed. "In the *bar*! And your frock, dear! I see, now, why you wouldn't have me with you to try on!"

"Please *don't*, Mumsy!" cried Nanette. "Will you *never* allow me to grow up!"

The blue-and-silver frock was certainly daring for a débutante. It was pure Paris; but Nanette's sweet shoulders were worth displaying.

"You are altogether too naked, dear!" her mother declared.

"I wear less when I'm swimming!" argued the reasonable Nanette.

"Never mind. Please wear your wrap, dear, or a scarf—at least during dinner."

And so the famous evening began.

Da Cunha had managed to get himself invited to the dinner party that included Nanette, and Jack sat facing him. Ensleigh, O'Shea, and I shared a bachelor table.

When the dancing began, I missed O'Shea. Nanette danced with me, but very abstractedly, alternately watching the door and the open French windows. There are few things more provoking than to dance with a pretty girl who wants to dance with someone else.

Da Cunha claimed her quite often and she suffered his public love-making in a way that nearly led to an outburst from Jack. The storm broke when O'Shea appeared. Nanette had begun dancing with Jack, but she did not finish. She dragged him across the floor to O'Shea, and:

"Please say you will dance," she pleaded. She turned to her flushed partner. "Then we will finish our fox-trot, Jack," she added.

"I hate to refuse," O'Shea replied, and his voice was very gentle; "but I came down to beg you to excuse me. I find that I must go out—on most urgent business. Don't be angry. I mean it, Nanette."

Nanette was not angry—but she was deeply humiliated. Every woman in the room had marked her descent upon the aloof O'Shea, confident in her radiant young beauty.

"I don't want to dance any more," she said petulantly, when the Major had gone, "at least, not to this silly band."

"It's an excellent band, dear," her mother replied, watching Nanette with a sudden maternal anxiety.

"They play such old stuff," Nanette declared. " 'Brown Eyes, Why Are You Blue?' is wildly out of date. They are liable to break into 'Rock of Ages' almost any minute!"

"Then what do you want to do?"

"I want to drive up to Gabriel's and dance to the Savoy band."

"Nanette!"—her mother spoke sharply—"I have already told you that I absolutely refuse. You heard what your father said?"

"No, Mumsy, I didn't," Nanette replied. "*You* told me. I would like to ask Pop."

But "Pop" had retired with a *Financial News* and three old copies of the *Morning Post.*

"Then I'm going to bed," Nanette announced. "I have a headache."

She turned and walked from the ballroom. Da Cunha detained her in the doorway, but only for a moment. Then he crossed the floor and went out on to the terrace. A few minutes later I strolled up to my room to get a pipe. The window was open, and I lingered in the dark for a moment, held by the moon-magic of the night. As I stood there, I heard a soft call:

"Nanette!"

Nanette's room was below and to the left of mine. I looked out. I could see a slender silvery figure leaning over the balcony.

"Is that you, Gabriel?"

"Yes, dear."

"In five minutes!"

CHAPTER VI
THE BUNGALOW IN THE HILLS

PERSONALITY IS A QUEER thing. Nobody has quite defined it yet. In my wild quest of a plan to save Nanette from herself, without letting her mother know and without compromising her, I came straight to what looked to me like an inevitable decision—I decided to tell O'Shea.

What I thought he could do that I couldn't do alone, God knows; but the Guards used to feel like that about him.

One fear I had: that he should have started out on whatever mysterious business called him. I raced across to his room. It was in darkness. I went hareing down to the lounge. Dancing was in full swing; no sign of O'Shea. I grabbed the hall porter.

"Has Major O'Shea gone out?"

"No, sir. Not this way."

I turned, hope reborn—and there stood O'Shea reading a note that a chambermaid had just handed to him!

"O'Shea!" I cried.

He glanced up. His face was very stern. His eyes glinted icily.

"Go and get Kelton," he said. "Bring him here—alone."

"But Nanette——"

"I know all about Nanette. Bring Kelton to me."

I ran. I was under orders. But it was a service of love.

Jack was in the bar—quite alone. He looked at me in a lowering way.

"Nanette's in danger," I said briefly. He jumped up. "Come quickly."

When we got to the hall porter's sanctum, and he saw who was waiting, he pulled up with a jerk.

"What the hell has *he* got to do with it?" he demanded.

"Mr. Kelton!"

O'Shea was watching him.

"Well, what is it?"

"This!" O'Shea handed him the note. "You read it, too, Decies."

Jack and I read together:

Have gone to Gabriel's bungalow to dance. If you get this in time, will you join us?

Nanette.

Jack crushed the paper into a ball.

"My God! The little fool!" he said. "Why did she send this to *you*?"

O'Shea stared the angry lover down, then:

"Because she is very young," he answered, without one note of anger. "Don't blame her, Kelton—and don't blame me. Blame the customs of to-day. Leave me out. *You* are going to save her from Da Cunha."

"Has she started?"

"I fear so."

"Then where's the chance? That swine has a Farman racer!"

"True, but he can't race at night on those roads. It will take him half an hour."

"We have no car!"

"We don't need one. I happen to know a route—a mere goat track—by which we can climb to the bungalow almost as quickly as he can drive there."

"You mean it?" asked Jack hoarsely.

"As it happens, I was about to take a stroll in that direction when this note reached me."

"Come on!" said Jack.

———⋅◆⋅———

I have the haziest recollection of that appalling climb. O'Shea knew the way like the palm of his hand. Under a sickle moon that looked so near in its white purity one almost felt one could reach up and grasp it, we climbed, panting and sweating. From the gardens of the valley we broke up through banana plantations where the great bursting pods banged our heads as we stooped to follow that tireless guide. We scaled a sheer hillside steep as a roof. We crawled along a path less than a yard wide, with a gorge yawning hundreds of feet below in which the vineyards shrank to a close green carpet.

We came to the red earth of the uplands. Our feet sank in it as in moss. Pines barred our way, rank on rank. Away to the left, below, beyond, the still sea shone like lapis lazuli.

"Ssh! Quiet!" O'Shea ordered.

We pulled up. I looked at Jack. He might recently have come out of the hot-room in a Turkish bath. His collar was a mere farce; a loop of exhausted linen. I believe I was no more spruce. I looked at O'Shea. That remarkable man appeared to be as well-dressed as usual.

"Single file," he commanded. "Not a sound."

We crept on, breathing heavily; and presently, through those sentinel pines on the crest, it reached us—the music of the Savoy orchestra, playing in a distant Strand!

"Thank God! We are in time!" said O'Shea.

We sighted Da Cunha's bungalow through the thinning trees. Lights shone out from three tall windows fronting on an L-shaped stoop. The windows were open, and O'Shea made his dispositions.

"Kelton," he directed, "take the window on your right front. Keep out of sight. Wait your moment. Time it. We shall not interfere." He held out his hand. "This is your chance. Make the most of it."

Jack grasped the extended hand, and:

"Thank you, sir!" he said.

He went off through the pines, stooping warily.

We gave him time to reach his post; then O'Shea and I made a detour and crept up on to the veranda so that we looked into Da Cunha's bungalow from a window opposite to that which concealed Jack.

The room was sparsely furnished. It had a polished floor from which the few rugs had been removed. There was champagne in an ice bucket on a buffet. There was the most elaborate and costly wireless set I had ever beheld. A Moorish lamp hanging from the beamed ceiling gave light. I could see two good pictures—both nudes—and a long, deep, cushioned divan. At the Savoy, they were playing Jerome Kern's "Who," and Nanette and Da Cunha were dancing to it.

I have said that the none-such danced perfectly. His dancing on this night was inspired—inspired by passion. He did not merely hold Nanette, he enveloped her; with his arms, with his ardent, lascivious eyes.

She swam into view and out of view like a dream-nymph hypnotized by a satyr. Her expression was indefinable as I saw it. A sort of exaltation was there, born of adventure and sensuous music. I could not know whether she had tasted the wine; but there was a dawning doubt, too, a doubt of herself that was not yet fear.

Then the music ceased, and we heard remote applause.

Da Cunha disconnected the set and led Nanette to the divan. He seated himself beside her, smiled, and put his arm around her bare shoulders. She made a little whimsical grimace, but did not protest. Then she glanced at him quickly—and he stooped and kissed her. It was a lingering kiss, which she ended by pushing him away.

Their conversation reached us as a mere murmur; but Nanette imperatively negatived further advances and pointed in the direction of the buffet. Da Cunha shrugged, smiled, and crossed to the ice bucket.

I had both fists so tightly clenched that they hurt; but O'Shea's hand held my wrist like a human manacle. Jack's inaction astounded me. Then, under the urge of O'Shea's iron restraint, I began to think. After all, poor Jack held no rights over Nanette, and he was too unworldly to grasp the inwardness of this scene. She had suffered Da Cunha's kiss. Jack was still waiting for his cue.

It came shortly after Da Cunha returned with two beaded glasses. I had watched Nanette whilst the man had poured out the wine; and I knew that, at last, pique, rebellion, having died their natural deaths, she realized her position.

He set the glasses on a little coffee table and drew it beside the divan. Nanette asked him to connect up with the Savoy again. He shook his head and smilingly handed her one of the glasses. She put it down, untouched. Da Cunha drained the other, replaced it on the table, and, suddenly throwing himself on his knees, clasped the girl in eager arms and burst into a torrent of passionate speech.

Nanette shrank back on the divan. Da Cunha followed her. He kissed her hands, her arms, her shoulders. He devoured her with his lips.

She writhed in his clasp, uttered a half-stifled cry, and wrenching one arm free, tried to thrust him away.

Then Jack came in.

He covered the course in four running strides, stooped, seized Da Cunha around the neck, and jerked him on to his feet. Whereon followed—catastrophe.

Jack slipped on the polished floor, stumbled, tried to recover—and fell.

Da Cunha twisted about and kicked him above the left temple.

He lay prone.

"Jack!" cried Nanette. "Jack!"

O'Shea's grip on my wrist was like a vise.

"Wait," he said. "The boy's down but he's not out!"

O'Shea was right. Nanette's voice recalled him. Da Cunha wore only light dancing shoes.

Jack rolled over, avoided a second swinging kick, and came to his feet, shaking his tawny head like a terrier with a flea in his ear.

"Jack!" cried Nanette again.

She crouched on the divan, wide-eyed. Her shoulder strap had slipped; and Nanette will never know how beautiful I know she is. Even as I saw, guiltily, she readjusted it—and the fight started.

Blood was trickling into Jack's eyes. He kept dodging and trying to clear his sight. It upset his judgment, beyond a doubt; added to which his skull must have been humming like a beehive. Remember, too, the climb he had put in.

To my intense annoyance, the none-such proved able to box as well as he danced and kicked. He took all a trained fighter's advantage of Jack's double handicap. Some punishment came his way, but it was not heavy—and he kept registering killing body blows on his opponent. Jack might have planted a lucky one before it was too late. But Nanette defeated him.

"Jack!" she cried, a sob in her voice. "Don't let him *beat* you!"

Half-dazed, the boy paused, dropped his hands—and Da Cunha recorded a tremendous right well below the belt. Jack went down—to stay.

"The dirty swine!" I exclaimed.

O'Shea slipped a revolver into my hand.

"I don't think there are any servants about to-night," he said. "But see that I'm not interrupted."

He stepped in through the open window, twirling his monocle on its black ribbon. It was not pose; it was nerves. The man was human. He was fighting for composure.

Da Cunha faced him, and:

"*You!*" came, as a sort of rapturous sigh, from the divan.

The two men confronted each other for an electric moment; then:

"You are a very dirty fighter, Da Cunha," said O'Shea smoothly. "But, as you are probably tired, I suggest that you give me the black dispatch-box that you have locked in your bedroom—and we will say no more about it."

Da Cunha's expression became complicated. My own brain was revolving like a merry-go-round. This sudden revelation was too much for me—that Da Cunha was a Red agent!

"Go to hell!" was the reply. "Who are you?"

"You are very forgetful," said O'Shea.

As he spoke, he reached out a long, lazy left. It looked effortless, but it was perfectly timed, perfectly measured. It started in the ball of his suddenly rigid right foot and from there carried every amp. of energy in his body to the point of Da Cunha's jaw.

There was a pleasant snapping sound. Da Cunha went down like a poleaxed ox.

Nanette sat silent, a second Niobe.

"Decies!" cried O'Shea. "The revolver! We have no time to waste!"

I ran in, passing the weapon to him.

"Attend to Kelton," he directed. "We must get him away."

He crossed to a door right of the divan and went into a room beyond, which was dimly lighted.

"Mr. Decies——" Nanette began.

Came the sound of a pistol shot... a second! There followed a splintering crash. Nanette leapt to her feet, and turned—as O'Shea came out again, carrying a small black dispatch-box. He put it on the coffee table.

Jack stirred and groaned. Nanette's gaze never left O'Shea. And now, timidly approaching him:

"I was mad," she whispered. "Oh, thank you!" She swayed and sank into his arms, her perfect lips raised to his in offering. "Can you forgive me?"

He held her for a moment, very tenderly, looking into her eyes, then:

"I have nothing to forgive, little girl," he said. "You have been foolish, but I don't think you will ever be so foolish again."

Gently, he set her aside, and:

"Decies," said he, "lend a hand with Kelton. We will borrow the Farman."

CHAPTER VII
A SHORT NOTE

WONDERFUL TO RELATE, WE managed to keep secret the story of Nanette's indiscretion. Her mother never knew that she had left her room. And it was toward dusk of the following day that the first act of the tragi-comedy came to a close.

To Ensleigh's inquiries touching my disappearance from the dance, I had returned evasive replies. Jack kept his room, for good and sufficient reasons, and O'Shea had gone into the town early and had not come back. Nanette remained invisible.

For all the glory of the Madeiran sunshine and the wonder of the flowers, black depression sat heavily upon us.

I was lounging on the terrace at about six o'clock wondering what Nanette was doing and whether her mother suspected anything, when O'Shea suddenly walked out to me.

"Hello!" I cried. "I thought you had gone for good!"

"No," he answered musingly, "not yet."

He sank into a chair, as though dog weary.

"Had a hard day?" I asked.

"Fairly," he replied; "but I've done my job. I suspect there are harder to come." He paused, then: "Have you seen Nanette?" he asked.

"No," I stared at him. "O'Shea, tell me if you resent my frankness—but that girl's madly in love with you."

"I don't resent it, Decies," he answered. "I know she thinks she is. But Nanette is very young. There is something you don't know—that nobody else will ever know."

I looked into the gray eyes. But they were not cold: they were on fire! I drew a sharp breath.

"O'Shea——" I began.

He nodded, and gripped my hand hard.

"Yes!" he said simply. "From the first moment I saw her. I daren't trust myself to see her again. You understand? It's quite impossible."

"But why?"

"For many reasons. Thank God, *she's* young enough to forget."

There was a short silence, which is more memorable to me than many long conversations.

"What shall you do?" I asked.

He pointed across the bay.

Trailing a pennant of smoke in her wake, the greyhound shape of a destroyer raced for the harbour.

"I sail in an hour," he answered. "I can take care of myself, Decies, but Nanette is of an age when a—silly attachment might spoil years of her life. So"—he took a letter from his pocket—"I have done a cruel thing. I have said what isn't true—God knows it isn't true! Her pride will do the rest. Will you give it to her—after I have gone?"

The promise was made. I thought of Nanette's fresh young loveliness, which this man, who wanted her madly, might have taken as an unconditional gift. I thought of certain others I had met. I recalled that we moved in the year of freedom, 1927. And I wondered.

I have known some good Irishmen and some bad. But Edmond O'Shea would be a mighty fine advertisement for any race on earth.

Nanette came down to dinner, and I can never forget her expression when she saw O'Shea's deserted table.

My task was going to be a hard one.

I took her out to the terrace afterward. Away on the distant horizon I could trace a faint wisp of smoke.

"Do you mean," she said, and her voice had changed strangely, "that Major O'Shea—has gone?"

I looked at her, a sweet picture in the moonlight. And little Nanette had grown up. She watched me with a woman's eyes.

I handed the note to her. She ran to the library window, tearing open the envelope as she went. I turned away and tried to trace the slender smoke trail fading, fading on a distant horizon.

A cry brought me sharply about.

Nanette stood before me, her eyes blazing, her face deathly white.

"Do you know what is in this?" she demanded.

"I do not, Nanette."

And indeed I shall never know; but I know what it cost him to write it.

A moment she stood so, glaring at me. Then, frenziedly she began to tear the letter into tiny fragments, and:

"How dare he!" she cried. "Oh, God! how *dare* he!"

Whereupon she burst into such passionate sobs that it was agony to hear them. Dropping into a chair on the deserted terrace, she cried until my heart ached.

It was her first love, and a very big one. An O'Shea inspires nothing petty. But she had courage, and pride.

She conquered her weakness, and stood up.

"You are very kind, Mr. Decies," she said. "I am sorry I made a fool of myself."

Then she went in, walking very upright.

I spent a wretched evening, and when I retired to my room, sleep simply would not come. I got up, with an idea of smoking a pipe, but, first, I crossed to the open window. On a moon-dappled path below the terrace I espied a moving figure; and Burns's words flashed through my mind: "The best-laid schemes o' mice and men..."

Nanette was stealing among the flowers, collecting tiny fragments of the torn letter that a light evening breeze had blown from the terrace above. It was a hurt, an affront; but it was the only thing of his she had.

CHAPTER VIII
THE CALL

"TELEGRAM, SIR!"

I sat up with a start. Morning sunlight flooded the large bare room. Wild canaries were singing outside my window. Slowly, facts began to assert themselves. I had been dreaming that I was taking tea at Stewarts with the Duchess of York and Mr. Tom Mann, when Trebitch Lincoln had appeared through a window, holding a bomb in his hand. Now, I realized that I had read news of all in a week-old *Daily Mail* recently; but that actually I was in bed at Reid's Hotel, Funchal.

The radio message that the boy had brought up was crisp enough, but it effectually banished my drowsiness.

> Please call on British consul at once. Vitally urgent. Am holding
> you to our bargain.
>
> O'Shea.

A bargain based upon the survival of so old an institution as the British Empire is not lightly denied: I thought that perhaps my dreams had been prophetic. Nor was Edmond O'Shea the man to send such a message except under stress extraordinary.

As I hurriedly bathed, shaved, and dressed, I reviewed the position. There was O'Shea, homeward bound with a packet of letters whose publication would further Red anarchy a number of points. There was myself, George Decies, who in a neutral way had helped to secure these. There was Gabriel da Cunha, agent of the nightmare called Communism, nursing a broken jaw as a result of foregoing transactions. And there was Nanette.

Even as her name brought the dainty image to my mind, from under the open window came a soft call:

"Coo—oo!"

I crossed, struggling with an intractable tie; and there on the balcony below was Nanette.

To know that the most provocatively pretty girl one has ever met is madly in love with a better man and to behave sanely in her company is an acid test of what I have heard termed "British poise."

She shaded her eyes with her hands, looking up at me. Her arms were a delicate brown colour on their outer curves where the sun had tanned them, and by comparison ivory white beneath. With a background of flowers against distant sea blue, Nanette made a picture exquisite to remember in old age but disturbing to a comparatively young bachelor. Temptation is sweet only when there is a chance of falling.

"What a horrid tie," she said. "Please wear the gray one with silver stripes, as it's our last day in Madeira."

There was a wistful note in her appeal, and, looking down at little Nanette, slowly a memory came: I had worn that gray tie on the day we had met O'Shea.

I suppressed a sigh, "admirin' how the world was made." At eighteen, there are many things that even Miss 1927 doesn't know. There was one that Nanette did not even suspect. There was another that I knew of; but this not my own secret. I was unselfish enough to wish I could tell her.

"Very well, Nanette," I replied, and lingered, looking down.

"Are you going to swim this morning—for the last time?"

"No. I have to go into the town."

"I don't think I shall swim, then," said Nanette. "May I come with you? Or is it a stag party?"

Before I could reply:

"Please remember your packing!" came a voice from below.

Nanette's mother stepped out onto the balcony and looked up at me in mock severity. Seeing her, beside her daughter, I reflected that the lucky man who won Nanette would acquire a bride who would always be beautiful. "Consider well the mother of thy beloved," says an Arab poet. "In her behold thy beloved-to-be."

"Pop is doing his to-night," Nanette protested.

I visualized "Pop," sole occupant of the family table in the dining room, dealing with a solid English breakfast, regardless of flies, temperature, and the indifferent quality of the bacon.

"He has none to do, dear," was the reply. "I do it for him."

"But, darling," Nanette wheedled, bobbed head pressed against her mother's shoulder, "there are hours and hours. Please let me off."

In the end she had her way, and we set out together along the dusty road. There would be disappointment this morning down at the bathing pool, I mused, peering aside at the piquant face shaded by a Japanese parasol.

Nanette wore no hat, and I said to myself that if all the women who were bobbed had such shapely heads as Nanette's, the world would be very beautiful.

"Did you tell Jack you were going?" I asked.

"No." Nanette aroused herself from a reverie. "I forgot."

Poor Jack! And he would have sold his Blue for a smile from Nanette.

The road to the town is very picturesque; and I might have counted George Decies a happy man had I not known that my charming companion loved to be with me only because I formed a link with her memories of someone else. Down the steep slope we walked, talking but little. An old roadmaker doffed his hat, smiled, and bade us good-morning. I sensed his kindly, appreciative glance following us. Funchal is famous for honeymoons.

Past the gardens of the Casino and the flower-cloaked balconies of villas we went. I forced myself to think of my real mission. Common sense whispered that I should have driven down in a fast car. Sense of duty demanded that I should conceal the nature of my business from Nanette.

"Shall you be long with the consul?" she asked.

"I don't expect to be," I replied.

"Then I will go along and have a simply perfect shawl I saw sent up to Mum," said Nanette. "She won't like it. But *I* love it."

We were just about to turn into that steep and narrow street that leads to the square, when:

"Hi! hi! Hullo there!" we were hailed.

We turned. Bumping along in a sledge behind two sweating patient oxen, was Jack.

"Hullo, Jack," said Nanette. "Mr. Decies has to see the consul and I'm going shopping. Want to come along?"

"Rather!" cried Jack. "Jump in."

We proceeded to the consulate in the bullock cart, escorted by a battalion of flies with fixed bayonets.

"Meet you at the Golden Gate," called Jack.

He was absurdly happy when I left him with Nanette and climbed the narrow stairs to the consul's office.

The British consul was a quiet little official automaton who had buried his heart in somebody's grave and had nothing left to hope for.

"Good-morning, Mr. Decies," he said, and smiled rather sadly as I plumped an ornamental object down on the table.

"Good Lord!" said I.

It was Nanette's handbag, a frivolous trifle from Paris, which she had asked me to take care of as we got into the bullock cart. I had been carrying it unconsciously.

"You are early," the consul went on, "and I have not quite finished decoding a dispatch which I am instructed to deliver to you. The main point, however, is this: Major O'Shea arrives in Madeira to-morrow night, and——"

"Oh!" A faint cry interrupted him. "I'm so sorry——"

We both turned and looked up.

Nanette stood in the doorway, her blue eyes so widely opened as to convey an impression of fear.

"I came for my bag," she said. "I didn't mean to intrude."

CHAPTER IX
MOON OF MADNESS

FIFTEEN MINUTES LATER I was in possession of the facts—and faced with a problem.

"This chap Da Cunha," said the consul, "isn't Portuguese, in spite of his name. He's some kind of what-not. He has the biggest radio outfit in the island up at his summer bungalow."

"He's a Communist agent."

"I know," the other returned quietly, "but it wasn't my business to mention it first. He crashed in his car the other day and he's dry-docked for repairs in a house he owns down here in the town. I know the surgeon who's attending."

I did not contradict him, for I was reading once again the body of the decoded message:

> Arrive Funchal Harbour 2 A.M. Friday morning. Please meet me. Arrange for accommodation privately. No one must know. Letters have all been photographed. See Da Cunha does not slip away. Watch Arundel Castle. Try to learn if any associate of Da C. sails. Prevent if possible. I count on you.
>
> O'Shea.

"Not a ship has cleared for European ports since Major O'Shea left," said the consul. "So there's a good chance."

"He's returning in the destroyer?"

"I don't think so." He glanced at a list of shipping. "Although this dispatch came from her. My idea is that they intercepted the Yeoward boat and put him on board. She's due here at the time stated."

"Devilish awkward," I murmured. "It's late to cancel my sailing. I'm booked in the *Arundel Castle*."

"I'll step across to Blandy's with you," said the consul, standing up and reaching for his hat. "We can get you transferred to a later boat. Leave the finding of private accommodation to me, too."

"Do you know of any one associated with Da Cunha?"

"No. Da Cunha has property in Madeira, but he's rarely here. Nearly all I know about him I have learned officially."

We settled our business at the Union Castle agent's, thanks to consular aid, and, the morning growing insufferably hot, my friend agreed that something icy through a straw was indicated. When we arrived at the Golden Gate this theory proved to be popular. A party from Reid's that included Nanette's mother had arrived, and Jack was sharing Nanette with a stranger whose ancestors had known more about how the Pyramid was built than you or I can ever hope to learn.

He reminded me of my London stockbroker until he was introduced as Macalister. He had a real-estate smile that was not unattractive, and my first, natural impression was that he had recently purchased the island from the Portuguese and was running his eye over the property. Presently, however:

"And how is our friend, Gabriel?" Nanette asked. Then, turning to me: "I met Mr. Macalister with Gabriel da Cunha," she explained.

I forget how Macalister replied, for I was exchanging significant glances with the consul. A few moments later that competent official took the floor.

"So you are leaving Madeira, Mr. Macalister?" he asked.

"No," the other replied, sharing an appreciative look between the cigar that he had just lighted and Nanette. "I had hoped to sail in the *Arundel Castle*, but I have been delayed."

The consul put several more leading questions to Macalister, in a chatty way, but I rather lost track of the conversation. Nanette was in a mood of feverish animation, which I knew, from experience, meant mischief. The party had been over to Blandy's apparently, and had learned that accommodation in the *Arundel Castle* was limited. Nanette and Jack talked happy nonsense about camping out in boats and what not. Then I made an announcement.

"Somebody is lucky," I said. "My berth will be vacant."

This statement was received with gratifying consternation.

"You surely can't mean that you are not coming with us?" Nanette's mother exclaimed.

Two pairs of eyes I particularly noted at this moment—the heavy-lidded brown eyes of Mr. Macalister and the wide-open blue eyes of Nanette.

"Unhappily, yes," I replied. "Unfortunate, very; but I must wait for the Royal Mail boat."

There was a sort of farewell dance at Reid's that night. Quite a number of people were leaving in the *Arundel*. Nanette persistently avoided me; and I doubled-up with Jack in a scowling competition having for target Mr. Julian Macalister, who had dropped in after dinner and monopolized Nanette.

Once, pausing near me:

"Do you know what they call the crescent moon here?" she asked.

"No."

"Moon of Madness."

She laughed and danced on. Jack scowled. I wondered.

At the cocktail bar, during an interval, things bordered on the hectic. I have been honoured in the friendship of some of Mr. Macalister's race who were very courtly gentlemen. Mr. Macalister was not as one of these.

"Don't look so gloomy, my lad," he said to Jack. "It takes a man of experience to please a young girl."

Jack had boxed for his college and was no mean craftsman. I rapidly took in the powerful but fleshy form of Macalister and prepared to mourn his passing. He smiled confidently; but one could have got roughly about the same odds on a peanut in a monkey-house, when:

"Mr. Decies!" said someone at my elbow.

Jack was just descending in a leisurely way from his tall stool. He paused as I turned. The British consul stood behind us.

"A word in private," said he.

I grabbed Jack's arm.

"Come along, too," I urged.

He hesitated, then:

"Perhaps you're right," came with manifest reluctance.

We walked out into the lounge; and the consul handed me a scribbled note.

"Received in code to-night," he explained.

Detain Julian Macalister at any cost.

Jack had left us, going to look for Nanette, and:

"From O'Shea?" I asked.

"No. From Scotland Yard!"

"But he's not sailing!"

The consul met my gaze of inquiry.

"That radio set of Da Cunha's is very well informed," he said. "Macalister knew of this move before I did. He only cancelled to-day."

CHAPTER X
THE ARUNDEL CASTLE SAILS

I CANNOT PRETEND THAT I was a happy man as I climbed the ladder of the *Arundel Castle* on the following morning. All my friends were leaving, and the affection and admiration that I had for Edmond O'Shea could not recompense me for their loss. My only consolation lay in the knowledge that, unhonoured and unsung though I should be, yet, in a modest way, I was doing my job of work toward saving Great Britain from the Reds.

An inward-bound liner, by the time she makes Madeira, offers a ripe crop of studies to the psychologist. The gay Conrads, who have learned the truth of Leonard Merrick's unmoral dictum, "a man is young as often as he falls in love." The anxious-eyed women who have lost what their men have found. A score of flirtations and two or three intrigues, followed with interest by the midnight watch and reported in routine to the purser. The odd men out, too, are always rather pathetic. It was wonderful how many lonely eyes lighted up when Nanette stepped on to the deck. Even some of the Conrads prepared to change their minds.

Baggage was missing, of course. Nanette's mother had lost a wardrobe trunk, nothing less.

"Don't worry," said Nanette's father, in his imperturbable way. "It will turn up."

"It will be Nan's turn to worry," was the reply. "All her things are in it!"

Nanette, the irresponsible, had disappeared with Jack in quest of her new quarters. She professed to be the victim of a dreadful theory that her stable companion was an elderly Boer lady with gout.

Coffee-coloured boys were diving off the boat-deck; vendors of lace shouted themselves hoarse from a flotilla of small craft that clung to the steamer like wasps to a honey-pot; Portuguese lightermen shrieked amiable execrations at one another; nobody could find the missing trunk, nobody could find Nanette; Nanette's father said both would turn up—and the Bay of Funchal embraced it all with peaceful beauty.

When the last shore-signal was sounded, I found Jack beside me. He was plainly in a panic.

"Here, I say," he exclaimed. "I thought Nanette was with you!"

"And I thought she was with you!"

"When did you see her last?"

"When she went to look for her cabin."

"But she came back to fetch *you*!"

"She didn't arrive."

"Hurry up, please," urged the officer on the gangway. "You're last for the shore, sir."

Jack turned and ran in at the saloon entrance. I could see no one else I knew; so there was nothing for it but to tumble down the ladder. Reid's launch had gone, and I took the boat in which some customs people, office men, and others were going ashore.

They had turned steam on to the anchor and the ladder was swinging up as we drew away. I stood in the boat, searching the decks far above me, their rails lined with unfamiliar faces. From the white-capped, gold-laced officers on the bridge, I worked down, deck by deck. I caught a momentary glimpse of some folks I knew and waved automatically; but of Nanette's party I could see nothing.

Then sounded faintly a bell. Straggling boats seemed to be drawn astern of the liner by some powerful current. There was movement in the placid water; a swell rocked us. One could see the churning of the screw in clear blue sea. Renewed waving—and the *Arundel Castle* was homeward bound for Southampton, with mails, mixed cargo, several potential weddings, and a broken heart or so.

As I stepped from the boat on to the stone stairs and went up to the jetty, I paused, looking back. I was shortly to meet Edmond O'Shea, and the thought was pleasurable, but I would have given much to have been aboard the liner now headed for the open sea.

I walked up the tree-lined street, sighing when I passed the shop where Nanette had found that wonderful shawl. The square, you may recall, is planted with those trees that flourish principally in South Africa and bear a light blue blossom. In the sunshine of early morning it seemed to me that all the streets were dim with an azure born of the flowers.

Only two tables had been placed outside the Golden Gate. At one of them a girl was seated, her elbows on the table, her chin propped upon clenched hands. She stirred slightly, and I saw the sunlight gleaming in her hair....

I stood stock still. Then I began to run.

Nanette looked up.

She was pale. Her widely opened eyes were the colour of those flowers—misty blue. And they said, "I am afraid. I am ashamed. Don't be angry with me."

"Nanette!" I whispered.

She bit her lip and turned her head aside quickly; then:

"I was mad to do it," she confessed. "I am sorry—now. Please send a message to the ship. They will be frantic."

"But—your things? You will have to wait for a whole week."

"They are in the small wardrobe trunk. I bribed Pedro to leave it behind. Oh, please, Mr. Decies!" She clutched my arm and I felt how she trembled. "Look after me. I am so frightened."

CHAPTER XI
THE PHOTOGRAPHS

THE S.S. *AGUILA* OF Messrs. Yeoward Brothers dropped her anchor on to the rocky bottom of Funchal Harbour at fifteen minutes after two A.M. under a perfect moon like the crescent of Islam; a true Moon of Madness.

They had the ladder down in a trice, and my boat drew alongside. I ran up to the deck—and there was Edmond O'Shea in a white drill suit, more like John Barrymore than ever with the moonlight gleaming on his wavy hair.

We shook hands in silence, whilst his searching gray eyes looked into mine and mine told him all that I was helpless to conceal. Then:

"It was good of you, Decies," he said. "My message has put you out?"

"I had booked in the *Arundel*; but it didn't matter. My time is my own."

Indeed, already the spell of The O'Shea was on me. There are many names honoured in connection with the Grand Parade, but ask one of the men who knows what happened on the Retreat when Smith Dorrien sent for O'Shea; a company commander then, and only a major now. We all won the war, according to our own accounts; the old Irish Guards—what's left of them—would convince you that Edmond O'Shea helped us.

"What has happened?" I asked him.

He gave me the facts, whilst we enjoyed the hospitality of the captain who was delighted to have been instrumental in helping so distinguished a passenger.

"The original letters are safe in Whitehall, Decies. But I found pinholes showing where they had been stuck on a board—obviously to be photographed! We sent a radio to Captain McPhee here, and I doubled back. The mails will be watched at Southampton; but I don't fear the mails. Some trusted agent will carry the photographs. I wired headquarters for likely birds."

"Scotland Yard replied," said I. "One, Julian Macalister, is under surveillance."

O'Shea's cold eyes fixed me.

"Who's watching him?" he asked.

This brought me to it, and I gulped a quick drink before replying:

"Nanette."

His expression changed; then:

"So they are still here?" he said.

"*She* is still here."

The captain excused himself gracefully, on a plea of duty; and I told O'Shea.

"You think she overheard you in the consul's office?"

"I know she did. She admitted it."

"And so you told her—the rest?"

"Was I wrong?"

O'Shea stood up and paced the room a couple of times; then:

"I don't know," said he. "Let's go ashore."

Fate has playfully set me in some queer situations, but I can recall none stranger than that in which I found myself now. O'Shea, occupying a room in the consul's house, and engaged in private consultations with the military governor and others; Nanette, studiously declining to meet him—although his return to Funchal was the reason of her being there; Da Cunha, incapacitated, and only able to act through Macalister; the latter gentleman dancing attendance on Nanette.

"He doesn't know that I know anything," she said to me. "And he doesn't know that Major O'Shea is here."

We were taking tea on the terrace of Reid's; the adorably pretty girl who had "missed the boat" and my innocent self subjects of much inaccurate speculation. Two frantic radios had been brought out to Nanette: one from her mother and one from Jack.

"Please answer them for me," was all she had said.

"Nanette!" I looked into the childish blue eyes, in which, when O'Shea was mentioned, I had seen the woman-light shine. "I feel responsible for you. In playing with a dangerous man like Macalister you take risks which you don't understand."

"I'm going to find out where the photographs are!"

"Because of—O'Shea?"

She looked at me bravely.

"No," she lied—yet did not know she lied. "Because Major O'Shea insulted my intelligence. I am going to find out for my own sake."

I dined with O'Shea in the town that night. He was frantically worried. That Macalister was the man to whom the task had been assigned of getting the photographs to Red headquarters he could not doubt. But where were they? And how did Macalister propose to smuggle them through?

"Where is Nanette?" he asked suddenly.

"Dining with Macalister at Reid's."

"Damn!" said O'Shea; then: "Go back and look after her," he begged. "I can't stand it, Decies. You shouldn't leave her."

"She dismissed me!"

"Report yourself for duty. 'Phone me here."

I arrived at the hotel fifteen minutes later. The hall porter handed me a note as I ran in. I tore the envelope open in a sort of frenzy. This was the message:

> Photographs are on board a motor cruiser belonging to Gabriel da Cunha. I can't find out where it is. But Macalister goes in it to-morrow morning to Las Palmas and from there by steamer to England. Have gone with him to the Casino. Will keep him as long as possible. Can't do any more.
>
> Nanette.

When I 'phoned to O'Shea, I heard him groan.

"Send someone from the hotel to stand by her," he said; or, rather, it was an order. "I can find out where Da Cunha's boat lies by using the military wires. It's hell, Decies, but I daren't take chances. Join me here. But make sure she is safe."

CHAPTER XII
THE MOTOR CRUISER

THE GOVERNOR'S CAR, A Cadillac—tribute to the far-flung efficiency of American salesmanship—was driven by the chauffeur over what I took to be the edge of a sheer precipice. I inhaled noisily. Then we were gliding down a cobbled road that, serpentine, embraced a fairy port.

Nestling in a cleft, a volcanic chasm, its terraced roofs silvered by the crescent moon, lay a town asleep. Patches of colour, as though a Titan artist had thrown uncleaned palettes into the hollow, crowded upon and overlay the white walls. Green fronds peeped above pools of shadow. A beautiful auditorium, this town looked down upon the eternal drama of the sea.

O'Shea spoke to the chauffeur in Portuguese. His command of unpronounceable languages was not the least of his acquirements. The powerful brakes were applied and our switchback descent ceased.

We proceeded on foot.

Where a low stone wall prevented the traveller from falling through the roof of a villa some twenty feet below, O'Shea pulled up, grasped my arm, and pointed.

Displaying her graceful, creamy shape like a courtesan stretched upon blue velvet, a fine-lined motor boat rode in the tiny harbour. Lights shone out from her cabin ports. O'Shea unbuttoned the coat that he wore over dinner kit and began to twirl his monocle to and fro upon its black ribbon about an extended finger.

"There is Da Cunha's boat," said he; "and there, no doubt, is what we are after. But it looks——"

"As though Nanette had failed to keep Macalister?"

O'Shea turned to me, and his eyes gleamed very coldly in the moonlight.

"Decies," he said, "you remind me of an unpleasant truth: that if I succeed in this matter I shall be indebted to a girl."

"She will have done a big thing for England."

"I don't begrudge her that. It would hurt me to think she had done it for me."

For a moment I hesitated; then:

"I think she knows it," I ventured, "and wants to hurt you."

"Why?"

"Because you hurt *her*."

He stared very fixedly out over the harbour for some moments, but he did not seem to have taken offence. At last:

"If I had married very young, Decies," he said, "and God had been good to me, I might have had a daughter like Nanette. Even if there were no other reason, shouldn't I be a blackguard to think of her except as a wilful child?"

But I could find no answer. This man's codes were beyond me. Young though he was in the days of the Big Push, he had won a name that had outlasted those of a score of general officers and more than one field marshal. The fact came home to me and brought with it a great humility, that I was not of the stuff that histories are made of.

"Suppose we go and look for a boat," I said.

O'Shea aroused himself—for he had his dreams even as you and I.

"A boat it is," said he. "As I have no official status whatever, there's nothing for it but frank piracy. Are you game?"

"Every time."

We went on down the sloping cobbled street. Presently it led us through the heart of the little town, where shuttered windows told of citizens asleep and only a zealous dog broke the silence. This until, as we were about to come out on the water front, from a high balcony stole the strains of a guitar.

O'Shea paused, looking up. A dim light might be discerned. He glanced at me, smiled, and we passed on. Love is an art with the Southerners.

I have wondered since, reviewing that journey, during which both our minds, I think, were busied with plans for boarding the motor boat and securing the incriminating photographs, that no premonition touched me. "Nanette had failed to keep Macalister," I had said, noting the lighted cabin. Yet Nanette had dared to slip away from the *Arundel Castle* and to remain alone in Funchal. I should have known my Nanette.

Drawn up beside a quay, a red blotch in the moonlight, was a long-nosed French car.

"Da Cunha's Farman," I exclaimed. "Macalister *is* on board."

But O'Shea did not reply. He was starting out in the direction of the lighted craft, a thirty-eight-foot motor cruiser, very handy in smooth water but a dirty brute, I thought, in a choppy sea. Then:

"I am wondering," he murmured.

"What?"

"Why he is lying out there and not alongside? There is no boat at the stair."

At first, the full significance of his remark missed me. My concern was with the problem of how we were to find transport. Then, something in the quality of that fixed stare with which my companion watched the lighted ports, his poise, as if listening, prepared me for what was to come.

The tones of a coarse voice, raised hilariously, reached my ears, coming from the cruiser's cabin. A trill of laughter followed, youthful, musical. My heart missed a beat. I clutched O'Shea's arm.

"My God!" I said, "he has Nanette with him!"

Involuntarily, my gaze went upward, to where in cold serenity the Moon of Madness raised her crescent lamp.

O'Shea from the pocket of his light coat took a revolver. He placed it in his soft hat and crammed the hat tightly on his head. He began to peel his dinner jacket.

"I'm going for a swim," said he. "Coming?"

But he was not alone in the idea. Before I could frame any reply came sounds of loud laughter, a scuffling of feet—and I saw Nanette run out on to the after-deck. She wore a blue-and-silver dance frock. I heard Macalister call to her and I heard her laughing answer; but I could not distinguish a word.

I saw her raise her arms as though to unfasten the string of beads about her neck. She stooped swiftly, stood upright again—and Macalister was beside her.

There was a shrill cry—half laughter, half hysteria. Nanette disappeared in the shadow of the awning. I heard the man's voice, his heavy tread....

Nanette reappeared at the bow of the boat.

Heroism is always beautiful, whether it spring from love of country or love of man. The dance frock had vanished, shed like the sheath of a chrysalis when the moth is born. A silver moon-goddess stood at the prow. She stooped, once, twice—I thought to discard her shoes. Then, as Macalister came stumbling forward, Nanette dived almost soundlessly into the still blue sea.

And Nanette could swim like a seal.

Macalister craned over the side. For one moment I think he contemplated following. Then the bobbed head came up two lengths away. Behind the swimmer, on a tow-line of beads, floated a flat, square portfolio.

I glanced once at O'Shea—and that man of action was stricken to stone. Fists clenched, he stood, watching a girl of eighteen doing the work he had come to do—and doing it for *him*.

Macalister was hauling in his anchor. The motor started with a roar. Then Nanette saw us. She was halfway to the shore.

"Please throw one of the rugs on the steps," came gaspingly. "And go away! Start the car up!"

When, a few minutes later, a very wet Nanette, wrapped in a light top coat, confronted O'Shea, I don't know quite what happened.

"There are your photographs," I heard her say. "If I never see you again, at least think I was not such a fool as you supposed."

With all her dear bravado, she could not still the trembling of her voice. I saw O'Shea's pale face, and turned aside. That meeting was one I can never forget. Yet the details will always be hazy.

Macalister was in the picture somewhere. I think I knocked him down. I don't remember why. But I fancy it was not because of any attempt to recover the portfolio but because he grossly misunderstood the situation.

Then, I recall, O'Shea stooped, lifted Nanette, and walked up the sloping cobbled street under a smiling moon. He had suffered as only the few can suffer, to make her forget him. His sacrifice had been rejected by the Great Goddess.

Once, Nanette peeped up at him swiftly. I saw her eyes. Then she hid her face against his shoulder. I think Nanette was crying. But I know Nanette was happy.

CHAPTER XIII
THE GRASS ORPHAN

"Public men should never indulge in private correspondence," said O'Shea. "Such indiscretions sometimes lead to war. I understand that all Napoleon's social engagements were made by proxy."

He turned toward me, his arm resting on the rail of the balcony. There were times when O'Shea looked extraordinarily handsome. To-day, I thought he appeared almost haggard. In his spruce white suit with Madeiran sunlight making play in the waves of his hair, he had all that curious atmosphere of romance that made him attractive to women and unpopular with men who knew no better. But his eyes were tragically tired.

I saw him glance at a square portfolio that lay upon the table in the shadows of my room.

"Six photographic negatives," he went on musingly, "and twelve prints—as all the letters photographed ran to more than one page. It's odd to reflect, Decies, that these scraps of film and paper might light a bonfire big enough to burn up a whole Empire."

Odd indeed; yet I knew it to be true. For that relentless loom which the Arabs call Kismet had drawn me into the pattern of this human carpet woven of anarchy, love, sacrifice, and God knows what other threads. I knew; therefore:

"Why not destroy them?" said I.

O'Shea shook his head.

"My instructions are to deliver them intact to headquarters," he replied.

"Are you returning in the Royal Mail boat?"

"No. They are sending for me."

"Lodge them in the bank, then."

"Contrary to instructions, Decies. They must remain in my charge."

I met the fixed stare of his cold gray eyes.

"In which respect," said I, "your instructions resemble mine."

"And do honour to both of us," he added.

I lighted a cigarette, smiling perhaps a trifle wryly. When a wayward beauty of eighteen deliberately misses the boat home and her parents radio an eligible bachelor that they hold him responsible for her safety, one sits up and takes notice. Traditional English phlegm is called upon to do its best.

On the terrace above the bathing pool, a band was playing jazz. Below my windows a multi-coloured cascade of flowers poured down, wave upon wave, to meet the deep blue ocean. Sounds of laughter came floating up. Little yellow birds darting gaily from palm to palm appeared to find life a thing of song. I wondered. Was it Abraham Lincoln who confessed that he could mould men but not circumstance?

"It seems absurd," said O'Shea, breaking a long silence. "But do you know what I was thinking?"

"No."

"That, after all, Madeira is a very lonely island."

He stared at me fixedly, until:

"What do you mean exactly?" I asked.

"Decies," he said, "the Reds have had a nasty set-back in England. But there's propaganda there"—he pointed to the portfolio—"for which Moscow would pay a substantial fortune. They have forty-eight hours to act."

"But only two agents in the island—one out of the ring."

"Gabriel da Cunha has a mysterious radio set in his bungalow. He will be in touch with his chief—and his chief is a dangerously clever man."

The official records of the Irish Guards afford sufficient credentials for the courage of Major Edmond O'Shea. He was watching me with that close regard which seemed to concern itself with one's subconscious self, so pointedly did it penetrate; and, rather fatuously:

"You are surely not nervous about your charge?" I queried.

He continued to watch me for a moment, then:

"No," he replied, and his expression grew abstracted. "Oddly enough, I was thinking of yours."

He turned aside, toying with the black-rimmed monocle that he rarely wore unless he were annoyed. At the Guards' depot in Essex it used to be said that the appearance on parade of O'Shea wearing his monocle made bayonets rattle.

Precisely what he had in mind I found myself at a loss to imagine, and before I had time to ask:

"Please, are you at home?" cried a voice from below.

I crossed to my balcony and looked down.

Nanette stood on the terrace. The sunshine made a glory of her tousled head as she laughed up at me. A stout German seated near by in a cane lounge-chair found his attention engrossed by the unashamed beauty of a pair of slim legs that had suddenly interfered with his view of the bay. They were delicately sunburned to the knees, which—the brevity of modern frocks and a habit of going stockingless had forced me to learn—were dimpled. One suspects that Cleopatra had dimpled knees.

"Yes, Nanette," said I. "Where have you been?"

"Bathing. You should know that, Mr. Decies. You are sadly neglecting your grass orphan!"

She looked very lovely. The German tourist raised envious eyes to my balcony, their envy magnified by heavily rimmed goggles.

"Please come down and join the party."

"Very well, Nanette," I answered.

But when I turned back and reëntered my room, O'Shea and the portfolio were gone. And I knew that little Nanette would be disappointed.

Presently, side by side, we walked down a shady path strewn with fallen hibiscus blossom. Nanette was very silent. An American training ship manned by naval cadets lay in the bay, and, at a bend in the path, Nanette paused. She stared out at the little vessel—"a painted ship upon a painted sea."

"One of the boys from the cadet ship is with our party," she said. "He's nice. I have promised to dance with him to-night. He's from Boston," she added.

"Has he got late shore leave then?" I asked.

"No," Nanette answered in a dreamy voice, moving on. "I don't think so. He just wants to stop. They are going to the Azores from here. Where is—or are—the Azores?"

"Quite a long way," I answered vaguely; for Nanette really didn't want to know.

There was small envy in my heart regarding the cadet from Boston. He was being used as a diversion by a distractingly pretty girl whose heart was not in the game. However, it is the mission of youth to learn, and the poor fellow would "learn about women from her."

I met him in due course. He was being lionized by a group seated around a table beneath a gay umbrella that cast pleasing shadows.

Nanette unblushingly monopolized him, and his joy was ghastly to behold. He would cheerfully have deserted his ship for her.

The sister of the British consul, who was acting as a sort of official chaperone to our grass orphan, kept throwing appealing looks in my direction. But I was helpless, and I knew it. A hundred times Nanette's glance sought the steps. And if only O'Shea had joined us, the eyes of the infatuated young man from Boston might have been opened before he doomed himself to cells for a siren's smile.

But O'Shea did not join us.

When I drifted down to dinner that evening, I missed him. I waited in the cocktail bar in vain. Nanette peeped in, too. At last, there was nothing for it but to dine alone. And constantly the blue eyes of Nanette, who had been "adopted" by a charming couple from the North Country, were turned in my direction. Always she smiled—but only to hide her disappointment.

The cadet blew along in due course, flushed with excitement, and was greeted by a very composed Nanette. Accompanied by her temporary "parents," she bore the young man away to the Casino.

I made up my mind to walk down later. But I was largely concerned with the absence of O'Shea. I hung about until after nine o'clock and was prepared to go out, when I saw him crossing the lounge. He beckoned to me, and:

"They are not idle, Decies," he said. "Da Cunha's radio has been busy."

"Have you picked anything up?"

"No. Conditions in the town are bad. But there's something afoot."

"Short of burglary, what can they do?"

He stared at me vacantly; then:

"I don't know," he confessed.

But we were to learn—and very soon.

A disturbance in the lobby proclaimed itself.

"What's the trouble?" said I.

Even as I spoke, the worthy man from Lancashire, whose wife had taken Nanette under her wing, came hurrying in. He was pale.

"My God! Decies," he exclaimed. "Did you send a car to the Casino for Nanette?"

"No!" I replied blankly.

"Damn it! I suspected there was something wrong!"

"Quick!" said O'Shea. "What has happened?"

The other spoke very breathlessly.

"Someone brought her a message—from *you*, Mr. Decies. She ran out without a word. Young Clayton, the cadet, ran after her."

"Well?" O'Shea urged.

"When I got to the door, they told me that both had driven off in a car that was waiting by the gate."

"Did anyone actually see this car?" O'Shea demanded.

"No. It stood out in the roadway."

"Then who brought the message?"

"A boy idling at the gate."

"You questioned him?"

"Closely," replied the man from Lancashire. "He did not know the chauffeur and only had a glimpse of the car."

"But I don't understand," said I dazedly.

"I followed," the hoarse voice went on, "but just this side of the bridge, where it's so lonely and dark at night, I nearly ran over Clayton! He was insensible. He's out in the hallway now! Nanette—has disappeared!"

Very deliberately, O'Shea adjusted his monocle.

"Decies," he said coldly, "why, in God's name, didn't you stick to your post?"

CHAPTER XIV
THE PORTFOLIO

BORN LEADERS OF MEN do not achieve leadership; men force it upon them. Here was a panic-stricken group, soon augmented by the manager and a doctor who chanced to be in the hotel. One was for communicating with the police; another urged the military; all were anxious to enlarge the news.

We were in a room on the right of the entrance, the medical man bending over an insensible cadet. O'Shea quietly closed the door. And I have since remembered how instinctively we all turned and faced him.

"Doctor," he said, "how soon will he recover?"

The Portuguese physician shook his head.

"Do not count upon him," he answered gravely. "A tremendous blow on the back of his skull. I cannot examine him properly here. He must be taken at once to the hospital."

"An accident?"

"But certainly, no! Foul play. Some blunt weapon. I suspect a sandbag."

"Shall I telephone the police?" the manager asked.

"No," said O'Shea. "Get young Clayton away as quickly as possible. Gentlemen"—he included us all in a comprehensive glance—"let us keep this affair to ourselves."

"What!" I cried.

But indeed, beyond that one word I could not go. Inertia at such a time astounded me.

"There is a well-known policy of war," O'Shea went on: "Masterly inactivity. We have no Service de Sûreté and no Scotland Yard in Madeira. A clumsy hue and cry could serve no better purpose than to drive the enemy into some more remote hiding place."

"But, Nanette!" I burst out.

Then I met O'Shea's glance. I noted the grim set of his jaw. I saw how pale he was.

"Your remark was rather unnecessary, Decies," he said. "I recently pointed out to you that Madeira is a very lonely island. If you can suggest any plan for locating the whereabouts of Nanette, do so."

Then I understood. And I think I groaned.

"There are so many roads they might have taken," the manager explained. "And what means have we of tracing the car? There are no traffic police in Madeira. Such a thing has never happened here before. Certainly not in my time."

"What villain has done it?" came in agonized North Country dialect. "Oh, the poor little lass!"

"Madeiran blood runs very hot," said the physician.

"No doubt," O'Shea agreed. "And Nanette is a lovely child. But do you believe there is any one amongst her acquaintances mad enough to commit such an outrage?"

"Why do you say 'amongst her acquaintances'?" I asked stupidly.

"Because *your* name was used to induce her to go," O'Shea answered. "Ultimately, she must be found. Her abductor knows this. Therefore he is prepared to make terms."

Came a rap on the door.

"Yes?" said the manager.

A hall porter appeared. Major O'Shea was wanted on the telephone. As he went out:

"Come to my room in five minutes, Decies," he directed.

The five minutes that followed form a blur in my memory. There were hushed voices. There was movement; a still figure being carried through the hall to where a car waited out in the scented darkness. Someone kept saying, "We must *do* something. We must *do* something," over and over again. There was a woman who sobbed with a Lancashire accent.

Then I stood in O'Shea's room. He was seated on the side of the bed.

"I was right," he said. "It's a move in the Red game!"

"What!"

My wild, distorted ideas were tumbled over one another by that statement. They fought in my brain, seeking fresh formation.

"I knew that if my theory were sound they would waste no time. That was Julian Macalister on the 'phone. It's the photographs they're after, Decies!"

Whereupon: "Thank God!" I exclaimed.

O'Shea raised his eyes to me.

"I forgive you," he said softly, "for preferring my ruin to Nanette's."

Certainly the swift tragedy of the last half hour must have numbed my brain. O'Shea had watched me, not angrily, for several moments before the full meaning of his words gripped my mind.

I dropped into an armchair.

Gabriel da Cunha and Julian Macalister, Communist agents, had triumphed at the eleventh hour!

"My special duties as a secret service officer end to-night." It was O'Shea who spoke, but his voice seemed to come hollowly from a great distance. "My resignation from the regiment must follow."

I spoke never a word.

"There is just one thing, Decies, you can do."

Then I roused myself. I looked eagerly at O'Shea. I think, in that dark hour, I would have crawled through the hottest alleyways of hell to save him. "Why, in God's name, didn't you stick to your post?" Those words of his would sound in my ears for many a long day to come.

"You can enable me to resign," he went on. "It would be preferable to being gazetted: 'The King having no further use for this officer's services.' "

"Anything," I said. "I will do anything."

A party of serenaders, playing gently on guitars and singing a languorous love-song, passed along the road below. Their voices mingled in perfect harmony. A sea breeze bore perfume into the room. And I thought that this soft island, set like a jewel above the brow of Africa, might once have been the home of Calypso, stealing men's senses.

"It may seem mere splitting of hairs," O'Shea went on. "But it serves my purpose, and so I ask you to do it."

He took up the precious portfolio, which lay upon the bed beside him.

"I forced the lock last night," he said, "but had it repaired and fitted with a key in the town this morning. I removed the seals intact and replaced them. Here is the key." He held it out upon his open palm. "Take it."

I took it, wondering and waiting.

"Now take the portfolio," said he. "You will find it is locked. Hide it where you please. But its security means everything to me, to Nanette, and to England."

"You mean," I began, "that I——"

"I mean," O'Shea took me up, "that *you* may pay this price to ransom her. *I* cannot. You have sworn no oath of allegiance to the Crown. I have."

"Good God!" I cried. "The decision is to rest with *me*!"

"As a private citizen you can choose between the claims of your country, in this very difficult matter, and the claims of a helpless girl who has been given into your charge. As an officer, I have no choice."

He spoke in a low, monotonous voice. But I shall remember every word of his instructions whilst memory lasts.

"You must not tell me where it is concealed. It should be in some place, though, that is quickly accessible."

"But, O'Shea! Are they sending someone to make terms?"

"They are. At eleven o'clock to-night."

"Why not have him arrested?"

O'Shea stared at me, and smiled. But it was a cold smile.

"Julian Macalister is coming in person," he replied. "News of this unfortunate occurrence having reached him and our mutual friend, Gabriel da Cunha, both are anxious to place their extensive knowledge of the island at our disposal. On what charge should you propose to arrest Macalister?"

"Directly he declares his real object, upon a triple charge of blackmail, abduction, and attempted murder!"

"And then?"

"Well, surely——"

"My dear fellow!" O'Shea stood up and sighed wearily. "Racks and boiling oil would never be sanctioned by the civil governor. Personally, I should prescribe them."

I was silenced. O'Shea was right.

"Under Portuguese law the case would take weeks," he added. "It would be adjourned to Lisbon. No. We cannot leave her in unknown hands——"

He turned, the sentence unfinished, and walked across to the balcony.

I knew that if she had never met Edmond O'Shea little Nanette would have been safe in England that night. And I knew that he knew.

Taking up the portfolio, I went out, closing the door very quietly.

CHAPTER XV
TERMS WITH THE ENEMY

I HAD NOTED A loose floor board in my room. With the aid of a knife blade, I succeeded in lifting it, revealing a dusty cavity. Here I hid the portfolio. I replaced the board and slipped the key on to my ring with others that I habitually carried.

That I was destined to be present at the interview with Macalister, I foresaw clearly enough. How best to prepare myself it was not easy to determine. Primarily I had to focus upon keeping my temper. O'Shea plainly wanted to be alone.

I looked into the cocktail bar. Two men whom I knew were drinking highballs, and:

"Hullo, Decies," said one, "what's this crazy rumour about your little friend?"

The words offended me. I suppose I was in a mood for it. Since the fateful morning that Nanette had missed the boat, many questionable glances had been cast upon me.

"It's what you say," I answered shortly: "a crazy rumour."

Then I went out.

I crossed the lobby and stood in the porch for a while, breathing the warm perfume of the gardens. A man and a girl were walking down the slope toward the terraces. He had his arm about her waist.

The open road called to me. Lighting my pipe, I set out. Drivers of bullock carts solicited my patronage, but I ignored them and walked on. I had no idea where I was going. I think I was merely running away from myself. I could not banish the illusion that Nanette was hiding behind some tree; that she would suddenly leap out at me with mock reproaches for my neglect of the grass orphan.

Twice I thought I saw her slender figure in the distance.

O'Shea was ruined. This was the idea that ultimately came to the top and stayed there. O'Shea was ruined. The blind love of a child-woman had wrecked the best man it had ever been my lot to know. She had stayed for O'Shea. No one suspected it. But I knew.

This was the sequel.

Lonely in my knowledge of all it might mean—when, willy-nilly, I should have surrendered the portfolio—I tramped on. A great, cold jewel, the moon lighted my way. By a stagnant cistern, green with slime, I pulled up. I had walked half the distance to the Casino.

This cistern was infested by poisonous insects with nasty habits in their tails and a social custom of leaving red-hot visiting cards. I turned back, scratching viciously.

A party homeward bound to Reid's in a car offered me a lift.

I thanked them but preferred to walk.

"... Having no further use for this officer's services." Yes, I could save him from that.

The hall porter said that Major O'Shea was in his room. Therefore, having a curiosity respecting Macalister, I took up a strategic position on a shadowed bench in that miniature palm grove which commands the porch. I told the porter where he could find me.

I had waited but a short time when Macalister arrived, in the pomp and circumstance of a glorious Farman. A chauffeur, whose pedigree connected with apes more recently than usual, drove the red torpedo in at the gate with much skill and even more noise. I stood up to see Macalister alight.

He entered Reid's proprietorially. He was in evening kit, wore a straw hat boasting a band of well-known colours, to which he was not entitled, and smoked a successful cigar decorated with what looked like the Order of the Garter. If he was nervous he showed no sign of the fact.

One has heard many jokes aimed at the courage of the Jew. Sometimes from members of his own race. In justice to one whom I shall always dislike, I wish to say that Julian Macalister, bearing a Scottish name, was fearless as any man who ever wore the tartan.

Caliban drove the Farman out into the road again, and I settled down with my pipe to await O'Shea's summons.

It came sooner than I had expected. Mr. Macalister was all of a man of business.

"Major O'Shea asks you to step up to his room, sir," said the hall porter.

Knocking out my pipe, I made my way upstairs. On the side of the angels though I might be, I found myself not wholly at ease. I rapped at O'Shea's door and walked in.

Macalister was seated in an armchair, a stump of fat cigar between his teeth. The band was absent. I presumed that he had smoked it.

O'Shea stood, facing me, by the open window. "I hope I have not dragged you from pleasant company. But Mr. Macalister here has presumed to question a statement of mine."

"Cut it out," said Macalister. "This is business."

"Mr. Macalister," O'Shea resumed blandly—and now I noted that he wore his monocle—"is not personally responsible for his defects of education. Forgive him, Decies. The facts, briefly, are these: You may recall that I recently placed in your care a certain portfolio, the contents of which you know?"

"You did," said I.

"My reason," O'Shea continued, "was that I feared an attempt by Mr. Macalister or his friends to recover this portfolio. I mentioned my fears to you at the time."

"You did," I repeated.

"Mr. Macalister," O'Shea turned to him, "Mr. Decies, here, has the portfolio and a new key which I have had made. The portfolio is locked. I don't know what he has done with it. Therefore your proposals are useless."

Macalister rolled the cigar stump. With a thumb and forefinger he removed fragments from his mouth—of what, I cannot say; possibly the band. Then:

"I believe you," he granted. "I never doubted your word. You're damned up-stage but you don't lie."

"Thank you," said O'Shea.

The tone in which he spoke puzzled me at the time. It was so oddly sincere.

"But, you see," Macalister went on, "I know why you've done it!"

O'Shea did not exactly start. But his glance, as Macalister spoke, was dagger-like in its intensity.

"You're an officer and a gentleman. The two aren't always twins, but you happen to be both. I've got to deal with Mr. Decies? If he lets you down, the disgrace is his. You're just branded a fool, but you save your 'British honour.' Am I right?"

By heavens! I knew he was right! And, studying the low brow, the small, Semitic skull, the gross person of the man, I wondered. If a Julian Macalister could read human nature so clearly, small wonder that the cream of his race ruled the Rialtos of the world. So I reflected.

"Very well, Mr. Decies." He diverted the cigar stump in my direction. "As it's turned out, I'm not sorry. You're sweet on the little lady who's disappeared. I don't blame you. I fancy her, myself. But business is business."

Only O'Shea's frigid stare held me in my place. I plunged my hands in my trouser pockets and clenched them tightly.

"Do not permit Mr. Macalister's vulgarity to upset your judgment," said O'Shea. "Also, make due allowances for him."

"I don't say I know where she is," Macalister resumed unmoved, "but I'm prepared to promise that she'll be home by midnight if you, Mr. Decies, will double on the major and hand over to me that portfolio!"

"One moment!"

O'Shea broke in so violently that he startled me.

"Well?" said Macalister.

"You fully appreciate the value of what the portfolio contains?" O'Shea challenged.

"Fully," I answered.

"You know what is at stake—on both sides?"

"I do."

"So do I. Therefore I am going to leave you alone with Mr. Macalister. Make your terms, Decies. I shall never reproach you. Communism is a powerful movement. To-night it conquers."

He walked quickly to the door and went out.

"Very pretty," said Macalister. "When he's fired from the Guards he should do well in the movies."

CHAPTER XVI
THE HOUSE ON THE CLIFF

I HAVE COME TO the conclusion that British honour is pretty good stock-in-trade. Macalister accepted my word that no rescue by force would be attempted. And, if Macalister accepted it, I think my promise must be a gilt-edged security.

At twenty minutes before midnight—the time I had arranged to set out—Reid's was moderately excited. The absence of Nanette could no longer be concealed in view of the fact that her worthy foster-parents had created something of a hubbub following her departure from the Casino. Hotel servants had been talking, too.

The arrangement had the charm of simplicity.

In a car containing only a chauffeur and myself, I was to follow the Farman. Any support must be not less than five hundred yards in the rear.

"But," I had objected, "although you trust *me*, I don't trust *you*. I might be held up."

"You can arm yourself if you like," Macalister had conceded. "And you will have the driver. Your friends, too, will be close behind you."

I had hesitated, until:

"Damn it!" he cried. "I want the goods! This deal is square!"

I agreed when he spoke thus. Slowly, I was learning my man.

O'Shea elected to follow alone.

"They will stick to their bargain, Decies," he said sadly. "We dare not take the risk, I admit; but Nanette is safe enough. They know how far they can go."

Past a curious group clustering around the hotel entrance, we walked out—Macalister, O'Shea, and myself. I watched a magnificent cigar being lighted in the Farman, wondering how and where Macalister found room to carry more than one at a time.

Then we set forth upon our queer journey.

The Farman led through the outskirts of Funchal, around the flank of the little town and out to that sea road which scales the frowning cliffs.

I am never at my best on roads of this kind. A squat red lozenge in the glare of our headlights, the leading car, from time to time, would disappear over a precipice. Nothing would obstruct my view of starry sky and the still mirror of the ocean far below.

Then, a hairpin turn in the dizzy path being negotiated, there ahead again the Farman would appear.

So it went, up and up, around bend after bend, until the bumping and jolting told me that we had left the road, such as it was, and were digging a road of our own.

We crept over a desolate dome of territory that must have been left behind when Atlantis sank. Upon our topping the crown of this blasted heath, I looked out ahead. I prayed that the brakes had been recently overhauled.

A long, curving, rock-strewn slope swept gracefully down to a sheer edge. And perched close to the precipice like a lonely seafowl was a little, dirty white dwelling—hundreds of eerie feet above the sea, approached by no perceptible path. I exhausted my imagination in endeavouring to invent a reason why any human being should live there.

By means of zigzag manœuvring, the Farman was brought to within fifty yards or so of the place. My chauffeur gingerly imitated the design. Then came the prearranged signal.

Macalister's arm was protruded. He waved his cigar like a field marshal's baton.

"Stop!" I said—and the word sounded like a gasp of relief.

I got out, turned, and looked back.

O'Shea's car had been pulled up on the crest. I could see him standing beside it, a distant silhouette against the sky.

I walked down to where Macalister waited by the house.

There was a low stone wall round the seaward end of the property, enclosing a tiny garden in which bricks were apparently cultivated.

And now I could see over the edge. I gasped. A wooden ladder, connecting with a platform that jutted out just below the house, described a jazz pattern down the cliff-side. In a miniature cove, below, a smart motor cruiser lay, her lighted ports like watching eyes.

"Send your car up to the top," Macalister directed.

I shouted to the man. And, as I watched him painfully tacking back against the gradient, I reflected that if O'Shea's psychology should prove to be at fault, mine was a sorry case. I fingered a revolver that nestled in my pocket.

The climb accomplished:

"Now," said Macalister, "you remember the conditions?"

"Perfectly."

"Halfway between the house and my car."

I turned and mounted the slope. Macalister whistled shrilly.

Spinning about, I watched. I saw two things happen.

Macalister's simian chauffeur leapt from his seat, stripping off his jacket and discarding his cap. From somewhere on the hither side of the building, which appeared to possess no door, three figures came into view. Two were men, thick-set nondescripts; the third was a girl.

And the girl was Nanette!

They held her wrists, but the moment she caught sight of me standing there in the moonlight:

"Mr. Decies!" she cried. "Don't do it! don't do it! I'll never forgive you! They *dare* not harm me, and you are not to do it!"

I made no answer. I had none to make. And so the men led her on until she stood before me.

She was pale, and so slender, between her burly captors, as to look ethereal. Her widely open eyes were fixed in a stare of reproach. My heart thumped.

"You don't understand, Nanette," I said. "There is Major O'Shea—and he wishes it."

One long, lingering glance she cast up to where O'Shea stood watching. I saw a flood of colour sweep over her face. Then her obstinate little mouth quivered. She lowered her head, and:

"I hate myself," she whispered.

"Now," said Macalister, coming forward, "give me the key."

I did so. He placed it carefully in his waistcoat pocket. Nanette never looked up.

"Hand the portfolio to Miguel."

The chauffeur was indicated. I obeyed, and the man handed the portfolio on to Macalister, who narrowly examined the seals.

"Senhor da Cunha," he said sharply.

Whereupon Miguel ran off, carrying the portfolio, and disappeared over the edge where the ladder was. So Gabriel da Cunha was on board the cruiser!

Again Macalister spoke rapid Portuguese.

Nanette was released, and the two men turned and went back to the house. She stood before me, with lowered head.

Macalister raised his straw hat. The colours of the band looked highly effective in the moonlight.

"Miss Nanette and Mr. Decies," he said, "I bid you good-night."

He was not without a certain vulgar dignity. He followed his brace of ruffians to the dwelling.

"Come, Nanette!" I urged. "It isn't safe to delay."

But, as we climbed to the waiting cars, she spoke only twice.

"They told me you had sent for me," she said, "because Major O'Shea—was ill."

"What happened?"

"Poor Tommy Clayton sat in front, and the man with me, who said he was a doctor, reached over and hit him with something. I screamed."

"Did he put his hand over your mouth to stop you?"

She nodded.

"Have they been unkind to you?"

She shook her head.

O'Shea waited until we gained the crest, then he got into his car and drove off. I followed, with an unusually dumb Nanette.

She sneaked into Reid's by the side entrance and went straight to her room. O'Shea was waiting for me in the cocktail bar. I entered very gloomily and he ordered me a double whisky and soda.

"They will have some little difficulty in opening the portfolio, Decies," he said, watching the bartender preparing our drinks.

I stared at him. He was smiling!

"What do you mean?" I demanded.

"I mean that I took the precaution of filing one of the wards before I gave the key to you."

But, even then, I didn't understand, and:

"What for?" I asked.

"Unnecessarily, as it fell out," he replied. "But my idea was to gain time."

"To gain time!"

"Yes. To enable us to get a good start before they forced the lock."

He slid a full glass along the counter in my direction, and:

"Do you play poker?" he asked.

"What the devil are you talking about?"

"I was merely wondering if you did. That portfolio which you have been treasuring, Decies, contains several pages torn from an old copy of the *Sporting Times*. Yet neither you nor I have told a lie about it from start to finish! Chin-chin!"

CHAPTER XVII
NANETTE IS CONFIDENTIAL

"Did you ever hear of Adolf Zara?" said O'Shea.

I shook my head blankly.

"That's the devil of it," he murmured. "He works in the dark."

"Who is he?"

He hesitated for a moment, then:

"He is the immediate chief of those Communist gentlemen," he replied, "whose activities have detained me so long in Madeira. One good thing I owe to him. I shall be returning to England with you in the morning."

"What!" I exclaimed gladly. "By the *Union Castle*?"

"Yes." He turned, staring at me in that coldly penetrating way which was so disconcerting and so misleading. "By a sheer coincidence, Mr. Zara is on board and I am instructed to look out for him."

"But the ship is full, O'Shea."

"There is always room for three more passengers in any British liner," he replied: "a diplomatic agent, a King's Messenger, and a pretty woman."

"What are you expected to do?" I asked.

"I am expected to prevent him landing!"

"But"—doubtless my expression became more blank than ever—"surely the authorities at Southampton——"

"The authorities at Southampton don't know in what name he is travelling. Neither does Capetown, apparently. They merely know that he's on board—with a false passport. He made South Africa too hot to hold him. Moscow's idea seems to be that another Boer war would add to the gaiety of nations. The Boers don't seem to think so."

He stirred languidly in the cane lounge chair and, raising his monocle, surveyed a number of ants performing mysterious evolutions on his white drill suit. It was very still and peaceful in the little palm grove. A faint breeze carried perfume from the gardens, a sound of distant voices and soft laughter. Outside the cool oasis in which we sat, shaded, Madeira sunlight blazed on a million gay flowers, and the low mossy walls were alive with lizards.

"Have you ever seen this man?" I asked.

"No," O'Shea turned his head lazily. "I haven't the slightest idea what he looks like. Unless I get some further news by radio, my chance of identifying this Red sportsman is a bad hundred to one."

"But you say he has a false passport?"

"So I understand. Probably issued in Paris or Milan or even New York, and in perfect order. Thousands of undesirables travel about the world annually with other people's passports, Decies. The appended photograph is the only snag, and you might be surprised to learn how easy it is to replace it and duplicate the official stamp."

Presently I went hunting for Nanette. My guardianship of this dainty, wayward ward was soon to cease; and whilst I lacked the courage to think about saying good-bye at Southampton, I had learned that for a man of my age and temperament the rôle of official uncle to a beautiful girl was no sort of job.

Tea was in full swing on the terrace, but Nanette was not there. I thought she might be on the tennis courts, and I strolled down the steps and along the sloping, flower-gay path sacred to basking lizards.

Halfway down there is a sort of abutment, overhanging the lower gardens and possessing a stone seat. Here, in a lounge chair, her parasol propped against the low wall, I saw Nanette.

Her little feet tucked up on the chair, to protect her bare legs from the ants, she sat manicuring her finger nails.

She neither saw nor heard my approach. And I stood still watching her. Quite mechanically she was polishing away with a chamois burnisher, but her blue eyes were staring, unseeingly, out over the bay.

As I studied the charming, pensive profile, I wondered, as I had wondered too often, what fate had in store for little Nanette. My more immediate wonder was concerned with the problem of how she had contrived to be alone.

Suddenly she turned and saw me.

"Coo-ooh!" she called. "Have you come to take me to tea?"

"Yes," I replied, walking down to her. "What has become of everybody?"

"I don't know," said Nanette. "I wanted to be alone."

"To think?"

"I suppose so."

I dropped on to the stone seat beside her.

"Whom did you want to think about, Nanette?"

She lowered her lashes, and polished busily.

"Oh—Pop and Mum—and folks."

I lighted a cigarette, and presently she looked up. Her clear eyes regarded me wistfully for a moment, and:

"You know," she said. "Don't you?"

"I am afraid I do, Nanette," I confessed.

"Isn't it strange," she went on, staring away over the sea, "that I should be so crazy about someone who avoids me?"

"Very strange," I answered dully.

When a girl thus makes a confidant of a man she has never kissed, if he knows the rules of the game he retires hurt. Then:

"I suppose I shall get over it," she said, and smilingly packed up the manicure implements. "We have to be on board at a fiendishly early hour to-morrow. I don't know whether to go to bed at nine o'clock or sit up all night. Let's have tea."

As I helped her out of the cushioned chair:

"I have some news for you, Nanette," I said. "Major O'Shea is coming with us."

Her eyes opened very widely; and she stared at me in a frightened way that I always associated with any sudden reference to O'Shea. Then she turned swiftly, taking up her parasol.

"Really," she said. "How often he changes his mind."

But as we walked up the long path to the terrace she talked animatedly. And glancing aside at her flushed face, I realized with almost a shock of surprise how very young she was—and how sweetly incapable of hiding the excitement that my news had created.

CHAPTER XVIII
SUSPECTS

THAT RUN HOME TO Southampton did not begin auspiciously for Nanette. Her happiness at being on the same ship with O'Shea was distinctly blunted by the presence of an official chaperone.

Her father had some sort of pull with the line, and by dint of industrious cabling, he had contrived to get in touch with a lady he knew who was returning from South Africa: One Mrs. Porter, a really formidable matron, deep-chested, heavy-jowled, and contemplating a sinful world through spectacles of an unnecessarily unpleasant pattern.

"Pop is mad!" said Nanette. "This woman must die."

Excluding O'Shea and myself, Nanette had come on board with a male escort of three devoted dancing partners. Lacking the society of Nanette, these were three very lonely young men, divided by a mutual distrust but united in their dislike of O'Shea.

Unreciprocated passion renders its victims clairvoyant; and each one of these three knew what the rest of the crowd at Reid's Hotel had never suspected: that Nanette only emerged from a land of dreams when O'Shea was with her. Now, to crown a troublous situation, Mrs. Porter presented a protégé—Captain Slattery. She made it pointedly clear that no other follower would be tolerated.

I resigned my staff of office with a sigh, and settled down to be sorry for Nanette—and Slattery.

O'Shea and I stood at the door of the smoke-room watching the coast of Madeira melt into a blue distance. Nanette, in a short, sleeveless frock, came along the deck, linked between two men, one of whom was Slattery. She pretended not to see us. But right in front of the door she pulled up insistently, leaning on the rail and pointing out something to her companions. Nanette knew she had very beautiful arms. But she wanted O'Shea to know.

He smiled at me, sadly, and turning, went into the smoke-room. The girl's dainty naïveté was hopelessly disarming. We sat down facing one another across a table, and:

"There is something I want you to do for me," said O'Shea.

"About—Nanette?"

"No." He shook his head, and that tragically hungry look came into his eyes that I had seen there before. "Don't let us talk about her, Decies. I have a valuable portfolio in my stateroom."

"Surely you will hand it over to the purser?"

"Impossible. Contrary to the rules of the game. The ship might sink. But a certain Adolf Zara is on board. Therefore——"

He paused, staring at me significantly.

"You want *me* to take charge of it?"

"Yes. Lock it in your trunk. I don't expect any move on this gentleman's part. He is stalking bigger game and therefore anxious to avoid publicity. But he *might* take it into his head to pay me an unofficial visit. I have a room to myself. You are sharing a cabin with a representative of the *Cape Times* whom, luckily, you chance to have met before."

"Very well," said I. "Of course, this man, Zara, will know you are on board?"

"Naturally," O'Shea returned. "His associates in Madeira will have advised him—although absolutely nothing to afford a clue to his assumed identity happened at Funchal. He is a dangerously clever man."

"Have you taken a look around?"

"Yes. Have you?"

"I have. But no likely candidate for the honour of being Adolf Zara has presented himself."

"I agree," said O'Shea quietly. "But I have an appointment with the purser in an hour's time. I am going carefully through the declaration sheets."

When O'Shea left me, I was joined by the journalist, my stable-companion; a substantial Scot whom I had met in London two years before. He proposed a promenade. And just as we started the faithful three came into the smoke-room, together, and ordered drinks. Their aspects were mournful.

Then, in a shady corner outside, we discovered the explanation. Nanette was coiled up in a deck chair, her charming head turned in the direction of her neighbour on the right—Slattery. In a chair on her left, enveloped in an unnecessary rug, Mrs. Porter slumbered soundly—and almost noiselessly.

Nanette beckoned to me. As I paused, she threw a venom-laden glance at the unconscious chaperone, and:

"I do not like you, Mrs. P.," she murmured. "The reason why is plain to see—and hear."

Slattery, his gaze fixed upon her, smiled admiringly. He had very even white teeth. Then he looked up at me.

"I hear that your friend is the famous O'Shea," he said. "I thought he was a movie actor."

The words told me plainly that this was another victim of the distracting Nanette. Therefore I forgave him.

"His appearance is certainly deceptive," I admitted.

"We were on their right at the time he was recommended for the V.C.," Slattery went on. "I was only a pup, but *we* saw some dirty work, too. The crack regiments always get the limelight, though."

Nanette glanced at him under suddenly lowered lashes, and:

"Please, Mr. Decies, lead me to a cool drink with lemon in it," she said.

She was on her feet in one graceful movement. Her ability to disentangle herself from complicated poses resembled that of an antelope. Grasping my right arm and the left of my startled Scottish companion, she moved away.

"Captain Slattery is so good-looking that he bores me," she whispered in my ear.

O'Shea found me some little time later.

"I have ventured to have you put at a table among strangers," he said. "Your immediate neighbour is a certain Dr. Zimmermann."

He stared at me.

"I'll do my best, O'Shea," said I. "Where are *you*?"

"At the purser's table," he replied, "facing one John Edward Wainwright, of Halifax, Nova Scotia. These two birds may prove to be black swans, but there isn't another query in the passenger list."

I experienced Dr. Zimmermann at lunch and later at dinner. Apart from his audible enjoyment of the soup, I found his table manners genial. He had been studying the neolithic fauna of South Africa on behalf of some learned Munich institution blessed with a name that only Dr. Zimmermann could pronounce and that I shall never attempt to spell.

My report to O'Shea was unsatisfactory.

"He seems fairly true to type," I said. "If he is not what he professes to be, he carries it well. How about your man?"

O'Shea shrugged in his curious way.

"He obviously knows Halifax," was the reply. "His line appears to be steam trawlers. Having unaccountably neglected the subject of steam trawlers, I am rather at a disadvantage here."

"I am equally rusty," I confessed, "upon the neolithic fauna of South Africa."

There was dancing on deck that night. Nanette danced with the faithful three in turn and with Slattery. Slattery secured more than his fair share because of the powerful backing of "Mrs. P."

Nanette was dancing with me, in a curiously abstracted way, when suddenly she grew animated. Her eyes sparkled. She floated in my arms lightly as a feather.

Following her glance, I saw O'Shea watching us.

When I had deposited Nanette with the guardian Mrs. Porter, I returned to find O'Shea; for he had signalled to me. He was standing just inside the smoke-room door.

"Adolf Zara is active," he said in a cautious voice.

"What do you mean?"

He glanced around the smoke-room warningly. I took the cue and looked about me. Dr. Zimmermann sat in a corner, fast asleep. Wainwright, the other suspect, formed one of a bridge party.

"Two dispatch-cases have been forced open," O'Shea went on, "by someone who entered my cabin to-night!"

CHAPTER XIX

DR. ZIMMERMANN CALLS

"YOU HAVE MY AUTHORITY to take any steps you may think fit, Major O'Shea," said the Captain. "I have received the usual instructions and of course I shall do nothing without consulting you."

We came down to the nearly deserted promenade deck. Three young men were doing a midnight route march there—and Nanette, coiled up, squirrel-like, in a furry cloak, occupied one of two chairs. The other accommodated Slattery. "Mrs. P.," leaving her charge in selected company, had presumably retired.

Slattery was obviously elated. The chairs were set very near to the foot of the ladder communicating with the bridge and the commander's quarters. Slattery didn't know that Nanette had seen O'Shea go up and that she was patiently waiting to see him come down.

We crossed to the rail, and leaned there, watching the clear water and the strange phosphorescent shapes glittering in its depths. And presently a slim bare arm was slipped under mine. I turned, startled—to find Nanette beside me.

"Please may I stay for five minutes?" she said. "Or do you want to go to the smoke-room?"

She stayed, and for longer than five minutes. Slattery had disappeared; and the threesome had terminated around a table decorated with tall glasses. We began to pace up and down, Nanette clinging to my arm.

Presently, as we turned, very timidly she slipped her other arm under O'Shea's.

"Is it true," she asked, "that there was nearly a mutiny at a reinforcement camp where you were toward the end of the war? And that a company sergeant-major called Meakin was courtmartialled?"

O'Shea looked down at her in his gravely gentle way.

"It is not true, Nanette," he answered. "Where did you hear the story?"

"I didn't believe it," she answered indignantly, "but someone told me."

O'Shea caught my side glance and smiled—the happy, revealing smile that had grown so rare. But after Nanette had retired, over a final pipe in O'Shea's room:

"Queer thing," he murmured. "That that story should have leaked out."

"What story?" said I.

"The trouble with a group of N.C.O's at that camp, which rumour would seem to have expanded to a mutiny." He stared at me coldly. "It was the long arm of hidden Moscow," he added. "We had agents of theirs in our ranks. Did you ever hear of it?"

"Vaguely, now that you remind me."

"The ringleaders managed to slip away. But it's odd Nanette should have got hold of the thing. Well!" He lay back on the sofa berth and regarded me with raised brows. "There is nothing more to be done to-night."

"Are you satisfied about Zimmermann and Wainwright?"

"About Wainwright, yes. He had been playing since dinner time. Zimmermann nobody seems to have noticed. How long he had been in the smoke-room I can't discover. We may safely count steam trawlers out, Decies. Focus on the neolithic fauna of South Africa."

"Shall you turn in now?"

"No," said O'Shea, reaching up to the rack above his head for a pipe and tobacco pouch that lay there. "I am going to spend an hour with the young gentleman from the Marconi Company. Radio operators are sometimes inspiring."

To reach my cabin I had to pass the smoke-room door, and, just as I came to it:

"Either of them is old enough to be her father!" I heard.

I stepped in. The faithful three alone kept a resentful steward from his bed.

"Whose father?" said I.

"Hullo, Decies!" the speaker hailed me. "Sit down and let's have a doch-an'-dorris. We were talking about Nanette."

"Oh!" I remarked, dropping into a chair. "What seems to be the difficulty?"

"Well," another explained, "she has fallen flat for that chap Slattery; and we were saying that he's old enough to be her father."

"He is about thirty-five," I hazarded—"a dangerous age for a girl of eighteen."

"Piffle!" was the retort. "Why, when she was only thirty he would be nearly fifty!"

"Have you pointed this out to her?"

"Rather not! Suppose *you* have a shot. You are well in with her ladyship."

"I should prefer to be excused," said I.

The profound slumbers of my Scottish friend proclaimed themselves to the ear as I walked along the alleyway leading to our stateroom. A sleeping partner who snores is difficult. When he snores in Gaelic he is nearly insupportable.

I undressed to a ceaseless accompaniment that I found the reverse of soothing. Slipping on a dressing gown, I lighted my pipe, determined to go out on the deserted deck; for the night was hot as Sahara; the sea a burnished mirror.

Off I went, and met not a soul. For half an hour or so I wandered aimlessly. When, at last, my pipe burned out, feeling sleepy enough to face the snore barrage, I retraced my steps.

Rounding the corner of the alleyway, I pulled up short.

Dr. Zimmermann had just come out of my room and was quietly closing the door behind him!

I stepped back swiftly. But I was too late. He turned and saw me.

He wore an appalling red gown and a really incredible nightcap. Through the thick pebbles of his spectacles he beamed apologetically, and:

"Mr. Decies—my *dear* sir!" he said, coming forward. "I can never forgive myselves—never!" He held up a huge pipe. "I did not know that you had a companion. I knock. I think I hear you sleeping. And I venture to come in. I am restless. The smoke-room steward is retired. I know you are a pipe lover, and"—he indicated the yawning bowl—"I have not tobacco, so, I venture."

I stared him fully in the eyes for a moment, then:

"Don't apologize," I said. "You are welcome to a pipe."

Opening the door, I stood aside for him to enter. My pouch lay, conspicuous, on the bed cover, but:

"I see it there," Zimmermann whispered, stuffing about an ounce of expensive mixture into his incinerator. "But you are not here."

Thanking me profusely in a thick undertone, he presently took his departure. I listened to his receding footsteps, then I stooped, pulled out my trunk, and examined the lock.

It was fast. Nor could I find a scrap of evidence to show that anything else in the cabin had been tampered with.

What was I to believe? Could Dr. Zimmermann really be the formidable agent, Adolf Zara? If it were so, he had cool courage enough to justify the faith of his employers. In any event, I determined that O'Shea must be informed without delay of this suspicious occurrence. Sleep was not for me.

CHAPTER XX
FOG IN THE CHANNEL

TOWARD DUSK ON THE following day—our last evening afloat—things began to move to that strange revelation which solved the Zara mystery.

O'Shea had been missing quite often. Several times I saw him coming out of the radio cabin, and he had had two long interviews with the commander, at the second of which the purser had attended. Then, having got into dinner kit, I was making for the smoke-room when I met him.

"Hello!" I called. "Any news?"

He took me aside, and:

"No reply yet," he answered.

"Perhaps the authorities in Munich don't realize the urgency of your message."

"Perhaps not," he said absently. "Let's explore a cocktail."

In the smoke-room we found Slattery and my Scottish piper; so we formed a quartette.

Slattery's attitude toward O'Shea was not friendly. I excused much of it, feeling the real cause to be, not professional jealousy, but Nanette. However, O'Shea was senior and Slattery never allowed himself to be openly rude.

I was seated with my back to the door, when suddenly I saw a change of expression on three faces. I turned.

Nanette was peeping in at us. She looked adorable in a dainty lace frock and I saw Slattery glance aside at O'Shea in a way that was twin brother to murderous.

For it was to O'Shea that Nanette was appealing.

"Would it be perfectly horrible of me to come in?" she asked.

"It would be perfectly delightful, Nanette," said I.

She came in, to the marked perturbation of the smoke-room. She sat between O'Shea and myself. The three musketeers, who had been talking loudly in a neighbouring corner, grew suddenly silent.

"If you see Mrs. P.," said Nanette, taking a sip from my glass, "please hide me until I get under the table."

Dinner that night was something of an ordeal for me. Dr. Zimmermann talked continuously about fossils, took two servings of every course, and generally seemed to be in high good humour. I think my own share in the conversation was not marked by any unusual brilliancy.

O'Shea's mood rather defeated me. He was by habit a lonely man, with a way of sinking into himself. To-night, this phase of his temperament, which had expressed itself in his evasive talk, for some reason I found irritating.

On the morrow we should dock. The identity of Zara remained a mystery. The result of O'Shea's radio message was unknown to me. And O'Shea had become a sphinx.

A group having for its nucleus the faithful trio had got up an extempore dance on deck. A victrola belonging to Slattery provided the music. Mrs. Porter presided over the instrument, and Slattery and Nanette did most of the dancing. A few others joined for a time and then retired, presumably to cope with the important job of packing.

I discovered myself to be the victim of a rising excitement. Something was afoot. I determined to find O'Shea.

It was a longish quest, but I found him at last, He was pacing up and down the deserted boat-deck. As I came up the ladder he stopped and stared at me, then:

"Hullo, Decies," he said. "Forgive my odd behaviour. But it's a race against time, and time looks like winning."

"What do you mean?" I asked blankly. "Have you had no reply?"

"That's it," said he, "and I can't afford to make a mistake. They expect fog, though. It may save the situation."

I was not at all clear on this point, but O'Shea immediately resumed his promenade and I perforce fell into step beside him.

"Zimmermann is in his cabin," I said.

"Good," O'Shea murmured. "Where is Nanette?"

The question surprised me. Very rarely indeed did O'Shea speak of Nanette.

"I left her with Mrs. Porter and Slattery," I replied.

He nodded, but made no comment. Presently:

"If this dangerously clever devil slips through my fingers," he declared, "Whitehall will disown me!"

And suddenly, as he spoke, an explanation of his recent behaviour presented itself. To the world he remained the aloof O'Shea; something of a poseur; a man unmoved by the trivial accidents of life. With me he felt that he could be real. He had treated the matter lightly enough, hitherto. But now, England all but in sight, and the enigma of Zara unsolved, he showed himself a desperately worried man.

"If I get him," he began abruptly, after long and taciturn promenading, "do you know to whom the credit will belong?"

"No," I returned, puzzled.

"To Nanette," said O'Shea.

This silenced me effectually. For what Nanette had to do with the matter was about as clear as pea soup.

I left him, toward one o'clock, promising to return. I had abandoned the idea of sleeping; and I wanted to change. No message for O'Shea had come up to the time of my departure from the boat-deck. The wireless operator on duty was unable to conceal his intense excitement. Just before I came down, leaning over the half-door of his room:

"Fog in the Channel, sir!" he announced gleefully.

"Good!" said O'Shea. "Go and change, Decies."

I managed to effect a change of costume without arousing my Scottish friend. He snored harmoniously and uninterruptedly. When I returned to the deck, no trace of mist was visible. The sea looked like oil and the heat was oppressive. I lingered at the rail for a moment, staring forward to where the Cornish coast lay veiled in distance.

Right ahead, I discerned a faintly moving white speck. Then I became aware of someone beside me.

I turned. The Captain stood at my elbow.

"No rest for me to-night, Mr. Decies," he said. "The Channel is a mass of soup."

"So I have heard," I replied. "What's that ahead?"

"I have been wondering," he murmured. "It looks like a motor boat—and right on our course. Excuse me. I might as well go up."

A few minutes later, as I rejoined O'Shea, the ship bellowed her warning to the small craft ahead.

O'Shea was in the operator's room.

"What's that?" he asked. "Not fog already?"

"No," said I. "There's some kind of boat in our way."

"Oh," said he. "Fisherman?"

"No. It looks like a pleasure cruiser."

He stared for a moment. I had never seen him look so ill groomed. His wavy hair, since he had gone hatless all night, was wildly disordered. Then the instrument began its mysterious coughing.

O'Shea placed his monocle carefully in position and lighted a cigarette. The operator adjusted the headpiece.

"Here it is, sir!" he said. "At last!"

"Excellent," said O'Shea calmly.

And, whilst this long-awaited message came through, the horn began its disturbing solo—and mist crept, damply, into the cabin. We had struck the outer fringe of the Channel fog.

At this moment I saw Nanette. She stood at the door, wide-eyed, wrapped in a furry coat. I ran out to her.

"Oh!" she exclaimed, and clutched me—"where is—Major O'Shea?"

She was trembling.

"Nanette!" I said. "What is it? He is there—in the operator's room."

"Thank God!" I heard her whisper. Then: "I have been so frightened!" she went on, clinging to me. "Mrs. Porter sleeps like a log—and Captain Slattery came to our room a few minutes ago and knocked. I opened the door, not realizing who it was."

"Yes?" I said, clenching my hands tightly.

"He was—insane. He said—he was going to kill Major O'Shea——"

"What's that?" came in a cool voice.

O'Shea stepped out on the deck. He held a slip of paper in his hand. The mist had closed down, now, like a blanket. Even the deep note of the fog-horn was muted.

"I've got him, Decies!" said O'Shea.

"What!"

"He sent off two code messages before my eyes were opened; and he received one reply. I don't know the code."

Dimly, through the fog, a queer, high siren note reached us.

"Major O'Shea!" Nanette released her grip and grasped O'Shea's arm. "Are you talking about Captain Slattery?"

The Marconi operator joined our party as:

"Yes," O'Shea replied, "thanks to you, Nanette! Only the Bolsheviks knew so much about our trouble in that camp as Slattery confided to you!" He turned to me. "I acted on that slender clue, Decies. The name of a company sergeant-major—and I was right! The *real* Captain Slattery is in hospital at Ladysmith!"

"Good God!" said I. "Then this man——"

"Is Adolf Zara! I told you he was dangerously clever!"

Then, muffled, ghostly, it reached our ears on the boat-deck—that most thrilling of all sea cries:

"Man overboard!"

Already the ship's engines were running dead slow. Now they were rung off.

Helter-skelter we went hounding after O'Shea—to Slattery's stateroom. It was empty. One of the lifebelts was missing. Out in the fog, that queer high siren note persisted. I thought of the white motor boat—and of Slattery's radio message.

O'Shea fixed his monocle in place. The sleeping ship was awakening to a growing pandemonium.

"Have you a cigarette, Decies?" he said. "I have smoked all mine. It needs a brave man to do what Adolf Zara has done to-night. If ever I have the pleasure of meeting Captain Slattery again, I shall tell him so."

CHAPTER XXI
A MISSING PICTURE

"OH, I SAY!" CRIED Jack. "This is topping!"

His admiring gaze was set upon a photograph in my portfolio of Madeira snapshots. It represented a slender girl, arms raised, poised in the act of diving from a rock into the clear water below. In justice to the beauty of the model and not out of any desire to fan my artistic vanity, I agreed with Jack.

The original of the study, seated on the edge of a table, slim legs swinging restlessly, surveyed the work with less enthusiasm.

"I look painfully bare," said Nanette severely.

"Can I have a copy, Decies?" Jack asked.

"Please say no," came promptly from Nanette. "If you want a photograph, Jack, I had several good ones taken in Switzerland."

We examined other items of my collection.

"Hallo!" said Jack. "Who is the sportsman with the toothy smile?"

He was frowning at a snapshot of Nanette coiled up in a deck chair. Seated very near to her, in smiling tête-à-tête, was a man whose white sun helmet cast a dark shadow upon his features.

"Captain Slattery," Nanette replied. "You don't know him, Jack."

She turned over the print, giving me a swift glance. Its full significance rather missed me at the time. I merely supposed that this picture of the man we had known as "Captain Slattery" conjured up memories of O'Shea. And memories of O'Shea almost invariably brought about sudden changes of mood in little Nanette.

Later, however, having induced Jack to telephone to somebody about something or another, she drew me aside.

"Captain Slattery is in London!" she said, speaking with suppressed excitement. "This was what I really came to tell you."

"What!" I exclaimed.

In the days that had lapsed since the disappearance of the notorious Adolf Zara, alias Captain Slattery, I had begun to share O'Shea's view that this greatly daring man had perished at sea.

"I received this note from him last night," Nanette went on. "And I don't know what to do."

Opening the envelope which she handed to me, I drew out a single sheet of unheaded, undated paper having a cutting pinned to it. The note read as follows:

> I learn from the appended picture that you are in London. If you can forgive me for my behaviour and will consent to see me for a moment before I leave England, put a message in the Personal Column of the *Daily Planet* and I will arrange the rest. I can never forget you—so try to be kind.
>
>   J. Slattery.

The picture referred to was cut from the *Daily Planet*, and showed Nanette as one of a group at a dance party—I forget where.

"How did he learn your address?" I asked.

"He didn't," said Nanette. "Look at the envelope. It was forwarded from the office of the *Planet*."

She watched me almost pathetically, and I divined the nature of the problem that was disturbing Nanette's mind.

"I simply couldn't do it!" she burst out. "It isn't as though he were really a criminal. He *is* a criminal, I suppose, in a way. But political crimes leave me rather cold. And, you see—he trusts me."

"Do you mean, Nanette," I asked, "that you don't want me to tell Major O'Shea?"

Nanette shook her head.

"Of course I don't," she replied. "I shouldn't have mentioned it if I had meant that. What I mean is—that I am not going to do what he asks."

"Yet he begs you to be kind," said I, feasting my eyes on Nanette's charming face which, now, wore an adorably wistful expression.

"I *am* being kind," she retorted; then: "Oh!" she exclaimed, and, suddenly silent, watched the open door.

Jack's voice might be heard. He was returning from the telephone downstairs and had evidently admitted visitors. A moment later they came in—O'Shea and an inspector of the Special Branch whom I had met before. He was a burly man with a rat-trap jaw, and I thought it probable that he could trace an unbroken descent from the first Bow Street runner in criminal history.

Nanette greeted O'Shea with disarming nonchalance. But the only person in the room who believed that she had not expected to meet him there was Jack. The detective, a peculiarly efficient man-hunter, as events were to show, smiled grimly and stared out of the window.

O'Shea held Nanette's hand for a moment, and then turned aside, twirling his monocle string around an extended forefinger.

"Come along, Jack!" cried Nanette gaily. "Mumsy will be tearing the Berkeley down!"

Jack was only too ready to depart. His admiration of O'Shea was something he could not hide, and, whilst he was no psychologist, this very hero worship inspired distrust—where Nanette was concerned. In other words, he was not clever enough to know that Nanette loved O'Shea, but he was modest enough to wonder how any girl could spare him an odd glance whilst O'Shea was present.

Nanette's vivacity became feverish. She literally danced down the stairs, calling farewells to everybody. But, finally, from a long way down:

"Good-bye, Major O'Shea!" she cried.

"Good-bye, Nanette," he said, and shook Jack's cordially extended hand. "Look after her, Kelton. She is well worth it."

"You're right, sir!" Jack replied with enthusiasm—and was gone.

"Now," said O'Shea, and fixed one of his coldest stares upon me—"are the snapshots developed?"

"Yes," I replied, almost startled by his abrupt change of manner. "The prints came in this morning."

"And are there any of Adolf Zara, sir?" asked the inspector.

"There is one. Unfortunately, his features are in shadow."

"Let me see," said O'Shea.

Once more my portfolio of snapshots was produced.

"This could be enlarged," said the inspector eagerly. "It is quite sharp."

"Does the face seem familiar?" O'Shea asked.

"Vaguely. I think I have seen him somewhere. But it's very much a case of a needle in a haystack. Of course, he's far too clever to go to any of the known centres—always supposing he's alive, and, being alive, that he's in London."

"He is alive, and he is in London," said I.

"What!" O'Shea rapped out the word in a parade-ground voice. "How the devil do you know that, Decies?"

In a very few sentences I told him.

"That settles it," said the inspector. "The rest is routine. Find the woman and your case is won."

O'Shea adjusted his monocle. It was a danger signal, but the Scotland Yard man was ignorant of this fact.

"Explain yourself, inspector," he directed, with ominous calm.

"Well—it's clear enough," was the reply. "I shall insert a paragraph in the *Planet*, and when Mr. Zara turns up, he will be met by someone he's not expecting."

"You will do nothing of the kind," said O'Shea coldly. "The assistance of the Special Branch has been asked for because of the facilities that you possess in cases of this kind. But on no account must the name of any friend of mine be dragged into the matter."

The atmosphere grew oppressively electrical for a moment; then:

"As you wish, sir," returned the inspector. "But you are going to lose him."

"I trust not. But even so, I decline to use this lady's name as a bait to trap Zara."

No doubt the man from Scotland Yard thought the speaker mad. No doubt he wondered why cases of this sort were placed in charge of distinguished soldiers handicapped by such preposterous scruples. But he did not know how Fate had intertwined Nanette in this affair so that at every turn success or failure seemed to lie cupped in her little hands. He took it like a good sportsman, however.

"Might I look over the other photographs?" he asked.

"Certainly," said I, and spread them before him. "The negatives are in the wallet. You will want the one of Zara."

But when, later, I found myself alone, and began to arrange my photographic gallery, I missed not one negative, but *two*. Search availed me nothing. The negative of Zara was gone, but so also was that of Nanette in the act of diving from a rock.

"Jack!" I exclaimed. "Jack must have taken it!"

But I was wrong.

CHAPTER XXII
PORTRAIT OF A GIRL DIVING

ON THE FOLLOWING MORNING Nanette's mother called. One great disadvantage of this era of freedom is that it has taken all the kick out of life. Without prohibitions there can be no thrills. If a pretty married woman had called upon my father in his bachelor days he would have immediately consulted his solicitor.

She looked more like Nanette than ever. Her shapely arms were sunburned, and (I thought) were very beautiful so. But, as Nanette had done, she declared that she was ashamed of her gipsy appearance. But she had come with some more definite purpose than merely to chat, and presently the truth popped out.

"Really, you know, Mr. Decies," she said, "I don't think it was quite playing the game."

I suppose I stared like an idiot.

"You know quite well what I mean," she added, and smiled in that way which was so like Nanette's.

"On the contrary," I assured her earnestly. "I really haven't the faintest idea to what you refer."

She stared at me very unblinkingly, then nodded.

"I can see you haven't," she confessed. "Perhaps you didn't think there was any harm in it—and, of course, I admit the excellence of the charity. But I'm afraid it will get her talked about. At least, you might have consulted me."

"Please—please!" I entreated. "Take pity upon me. You are clearly referring to something of which I have no knowledge whatever——"

"Mr. Decies," she interrupted—and held out a newspaper which she carried—"I am referring to the picture in the *Daily Planet*."

"But what have I to do with the pictures in the *Daily Planet*?" I asked blankly.

"Since you took the picture in question, the connection in this case is obvious."

Dazedly, I opened the copy of the *Planet* which she handed to me—and there, prominently featured, was a large reproduction of my snapshot of Nanette diving! The caption read:

> A charming study of a charming diver. No wonder Madeira grows more popular every season. The original photograph is on view in the Modern Gallery, Bond Street, amongst a collection offered for sale in aid of St. Dunstan's Institute for Blinded Soldiers.

To say that I was staggered is to convey but a feeble idea of my frame of mind. I stared at the picture until I seemed to see it dimly through a haze. When, at last, I looked up and met the reproachful gaze of Nanette's mother, I was temporarily past comment.

My innocence must have proclaimed itself, for:

"Mr. Decies," she said, and I saw her expression change, "I must apologize. You evidently are as surprised as I was. But this only deepens the mystery. Did you develop this film yourself?"

"No," I answered. "It was on one of several spools which I brought back. The Kodak people developed it. But——"

I stopped short. The truth had presented itself to me. One of four people had taken this unaccountable liberty with the photograph. Jack, the inspector, O'Shea, or Nanette herself. For I had no evidence to show which of these four had removed the negative from the wallet.

"Yes?" Nanette's mother prompted.

"The firm in question certainly knows nothing of the matter," I went on. "You see, I missed this negative yesterday."

"You mean that someone stole it?"

"Stole it or borrowed it."

"But with what object?"

"Presumably a philanthropic one," said I, very blankly. "Nobody profits—except the charity."

"It resembles the work of an enemy—if one can imagine Nan having an enemy. Unfortunately, it is a perfect likeness. In fact, it was brought to my notice by someone. Personally, I don't read the *Planet*."

"What does Nanette think about it?"

"She doesn't know. That is, she had already gone out when the paper was shown to me. She may know by now. I am afraid it will earn her a rather unenviable notoriety."

I promised that I would thresh the matter out, but as I had a luncheon appointment all I could hope to do immediately was to ring up the *Planet* and speak to the department responsible.

This led to nowhere.

The art editor was out, and apparently no other member of the staff knew anything whatever about the photograph—or about anything else.

I lunched that day at the Savoy Grill. So did nearly everybody who had been in Funchal whilst Nanette was there. The room appeared to be decorated with copies of the *Planet*, and my reception would have gratified Gene Tunney and overwhelmed Douglas Fairbanks. I grew stickily embarrassed.

Finally, I made my escape—and in the lobby ran into Jack.

"I say, Decies," he exclaimed, "it's hardly good enough. Nanette kicked at the picture from the first. Now you go and publish it!"

"Stop!" I said sharply. "This is the last time I shall explain the fact to anyone. But I did not send Nanette's photograph to the *Planet*. Except that someone stole the negative from the portfolio at my rooms yesterday, I know nothing whatever about the matter."

"*Stole* it!"

"Exactly."

"But when?"

"I missed it just after you had gone. In fact, Jack, I thought at the time you had borrowed it to have a copy made."

"Good heavens, no! She didn't want me to have it."

"Then the mystery remains a mystery."

"It's so objectless!" cried Jack. "A photograph like that is just good fun amongst friends, but one doesn't want the million readers of the *Planet* to see it. This defeats me! Have you rung up the office?"

"Yes. I could get no satisfaction. I am going along to the Modern Gallery now."

"I'll come with you!" said Jack.

CHAPTER XXIII
FIASCO

A CURIOUS EPISODE MARKED our arrival at the gallery. On the opposite side of Bond Street, you may recall that there is a block of offices and showrooms, occupied by beauty specialists, modistes, and others. Well, at the entrance to the gallery, where an announcement stated that an exhibition of modern drawings and art photographs was being held in aid of, etc., we bumped into one of Nanette's Madeira conquests.

"Hallo, Milton!" said I.

The young man, who had been leaning against the doorway and staring abstractedly across the street, became galvanized into sudden action. He gave a swift look at me, a second look at Jack, and then:

"Hallo, Decies," he returned in an oddly guilty way.

Immediately he stared across the street again. At which moment came a cry from Jack.

"Gad! There's Nanette!"

"Where?" I asked.

"In that window, on the first floor there. She has seen us, I think."

I followed the direction of his gaze. The window indicated belonged to an expert organizer of female hair. An attractive wax bust was visible but no Nanette. I turned to Milton.

"*Is* Nanette there?" I asked.

"I couldn't say," he replied evasively.

Jack gave him a venomous glance and started across the street.

"We can see for ourselves," he snapped.

I looked inquiringly at the young man in the doorway, but he returned my regard with so high a challenge that I wondered, checked the words on my tongue, and followed Jack.

We mounted the stairway to the first landing, and Jack threw open a door bearing the simple legend "Pierre" with quite unnecessary violence. We found ourselves in a discreet waiting room delicately perfumed. A stout French gentleman, whose wavy gleaming locks were a credit to his professional acquirements, greeted us. He bowed.

"I have called for a lady who is here," said Jack. "Please tell her Mr. Decies and Mr. Kelton."

"But there is some mistake," Pierre replied—assuming that this was none other than the maestro in person. "No one is here at the moment—unless you mean Mlle. Justine, my assistant." He raised his voice. "Justine!"

A trim figure in white appeared at the door of an inner sanctuary sacred to hair.

"M'sieur?" said Justine, and bestowed upon us a swift glance of roguish dark eyes.

"You are alone?"

"Yes, m'sieur. I am waiting for Lady Rickaby whose appointment is at three."

She bit her lip, suppressing a smile, and disappeared.

"You see?" M. Pierre extended apologetic palms. "There is no one."

"What's afoot?" Jack asked as we regained Bond Street. "That fat bird was lying. The girl gave it away. Nanette is hiding from us."

We stared at each other, badly puzzled. Then we looked across to where Milton lounged in the entrance to the Modern Gallery, seemingly oblivious of our existence.

"Come on!" said Jack savagely.

We joined the waiting Milton.

"Have you seen the famous picture?" I asked.

"No," he replied, "I haven't."

Jack made a snorting noise, then, paying a shilling each, we went into the exhibition. We found it to be far from crowded, and, indeed, the artistic donations were not of outstanding merit. Quite the most interesting exhibit was the lady in charge of the sales department. And, at the end of a ten minutes' quest, we sought her aid.

"Perhaps you could tell me," said I, "where the picture is that was reproduced in to-day's *Planet*—a portrait of a girl diving."

Whereupon the lady addressed began to laugh!

Jack's expression was worthy of study. In the eyes of poor Jack, anything touching Nanette was sacred, and this was the second time in one afternoon that inquiries concerning her had provoked merriment.

"I wish I could!" was the reply. "Really, it's most absurd. But all the same the publicity has done the exhibition a lot of good. Forgive my laughter, but, you see, we know nothing whatever about this picture!"

"What!"

Jack's exclamation was not merely rude; it was explosive.

"It has never been here," she went on. "Dozens of people have asked about it. But *we* have never seen it. The secretary 'phoned the *Planet* this morning and was told that they had used the photograph in good faith."

"But who sent it to them?" I asked.

"I am afraid I can't tell you," was the answer. "All we could learn was that it had been sent in by a responsible agency. Personally, of course, we are rather grateful."

In silence Jack and I departed. Milton was standing in Bond Street just outside the doorway.

"Good-bye, Milton," I said. "Let's hope it keeps fine."

"Good-bye, Decies," said he, jauntily imperturbable.

Jack glanced sharply up at M. Pierre's windows; but only the wax bust rewarded his scrutiny.

"I am beginning to hate your friend Milton," he confided.

"He is not so popular with *me*," I confessed.

"Come round to the club," Jack suggested. "This thing calls for cool reflection."

I left him at four o'clock. We had telephoned Nanette's mother, only to learn that Nanette had not returned. The whole thing was provokingly mysterious. It had entirely diverted my thoughts from the more serious problem of the capture of Adolf Zara. In fact, I could not shake my mind free of it.

That Nanette had been hiding in the establishment of M. Pierre, I no longer doubted. And that Milton had some part in the comedy was clear enough. Poor fellow, I regarded him in a more charitable spirit than Jack had at command. Nanette had been using him—for what purpose I could not imagine—and his reward would be small.

Some association between Nanette, at M. Pierre's, and Milton, in the entrance of the Modern Gallery, seemed to be established. But since Nanette's photograph was not in the gallery, why this association—and conveying what?

Nothing—in so far as my bewildered brain served me.

So I mused, as I drifted along Pall Mall. I determined to hunt up O'Shea, when, suddenly, I saw something which called me to prompt action.

A taxi turned a corner at the very moment I was about to cross. In it sat Nanette—and Adolf Zara!

It is in such moments of stress as this that vacant cabs magically disappear from the streets. No fewer than five taximen had solicited my patronage during the few minutes that had elapsed since I had left Jack.

Now, with a dangerous agitator wanted by the British Government disappearing in the distance, from end to end of Pall Mall not a taxi was in sight!

When at last one crept into view, pursuit was out of the question.

If I had been perplexed before, perplexity now gave place to consternation. The comedy of Bond Street had been no more than a gay curtain draped before a stage set for drama. I tried in vain to allot the actors their proper rôles. What part did the missing photograph play? How came Zara in the cast? What of Milton? And what of Nanette?

It was not far to my chambers, and I hurried back, with the intention of 'phoning O'Shea.

I met him at the door.

Those who enjoyed the privilege of seeing Edmond O'Shea in action relate that when things were going hopelessly wrong he would fix his monocle immovably in his eye and retain it there, contrary to regulations, throughout the hottest fighting. He was wearing it now.

"Hallo, O'Shea!" I called. "This is lucky! I want to see you badly."

"I came to see *you*, Decies," said he. "There is something I wish you to know."

Having opened the door and hurried him upstairs:

"Don't jump to conclusions," I began. "But Nanette met Zara this afternoon."

O'Shea stared at me incredulously.

"Where?" he demanded.

"I don't know where. But I saw them together not ten minutes ago."

He hesitated for a moment; then:

"Tell me all about it," he said calmly.

In as few words as possible I outlined the events of the day, terminating with my glimpse of Nanette and Adolf Zara together in Pall Mall.

"It is a blank mystery to me, O'Shea," I said. "I simply cannot understand what it's all about."

"To me," he replied, "it is equally, but painfully, clear."

"What do you mean?"

"In the first place," said he, "our friend the inspector borrowed your negative of Nanette."

"The inspector! In heaven's name, what for?"

"Because he happens to be a clever man at his trade. I declined to allow him to insert a paragraph in Nanette's name. But he was by no means defeated. He employed certain official channels and secured the publication of her photograph."

"With what object?"

"You recall the words that appeared under the picture?"

"Clearly. But the original was *not* in Bond Street."

"Quite unnecessary that it should be, Decies. Our friend the inspector was in Bond Street, however."

I think I was gaping like an imbecile.

"You are simply confusing me, O'Shea," I managed to say.

"Yes," he admitted. "No doubt the scheme is difficult to grasp. You see—the inspector banked on Zara's infatuation for Nanette. He judged it, no doubt, by the risk that Zara ran in communicating with her."

"Good heavens!" I cried. "I see it all! He hoped in this way to lure Zara to the gallery?"

"Certainly. He thought that Zara would probably come, first, to secure the picture, and, second, possibly to obtain a glimpse of Nanette in person."

"And you say the inspector was there? I didn't see him."

"I did!" said O'Shea grimly. "He was in an office at the end of the gallery—with the door ajar. The girl in charge knew he was there on some police business, but she did not know that it had any connection with the missing print. I gave him a crisp five minutes. But, officially, he was within his rights—and he knew it, dash him!"

"O'Shea," I said, "I can't fit Nanette and young Milton into the picture."

O'Shea's expression changed, softened.

"I wonder?" he murmured. "She has a high spirit, and, I am beginning to think, a keen brain. Decies!"—he suddenly grasped my shoulder—"how happy some man is going to be, some day!"

He turned aside abruptly, and walked into the inner room where my modest library formed a haven of refuge. Vaguely, as we had talked, I had grown aware of voices below. My man was one of the speakers; the other voice had been inaudible throughout.

Then I heard the door open behind me. I looked. And there was Nanette!

But, even as I was about to greet her, I checked the words. I had seen Nanette merry; I had seen her sad. I knew her moods of coquetry and of contrition. But, always, save once, I had thought of her as a child. I did not know her as I saw her now.

"I thought you were my friend," she said. "I thought I could trust you. If I had had one little doubt I would never have told you——"

"Nanette," I began——

But she checked me with a sad, angry gesture.

"You are no better than *he* is," she went on bitterly; "for you helped him. Heavens, what a fool I have been! And he only thinks of me as a *bait* for his traps!"

"Stop!" I cried. "For heaven's sake, stop, Nanette!"

"He was right," she pursued, stonily ignoring me, and looking unseeingly, miserably, before her as she spoke. "Captain Slattery came. But I had arranged to warn him."

I remembered Milton and his watch upon the window of M. Pierre. Then, abruptly, her mood changed. The blue eyes, which were so sweetly childish, blazed at me.

"No man, however bad he is, shall ever be lured to ruin by *me*. Tell Major O'Shea that Captain Slattery is laughing at him!"

"He is entitled to laugh, Nanette," said a grave voice.

O'Shea came out from the recess and stood watching her.

A moment she confronted him, then:

"Good-bye!" she said.

Turning, Nanette ran from the room. I heard the street door slam.

"O'Shea!" I cried. "Why didn't you tell her?"

"It is better she should think as she does," he replied. "Fate has done what I failed to do. Now she will forget."

I have often wondered, since, if he believed it would be so. I have tried, knowing the man's honesty of soul, to conceive that he hoped it would be so. What *I* believed or what I hoped I cannot pretend to record. But, at some hour past midnight, I learned that Nanette was unwilling to ignore the promptings of her heart.

Dejectedly, I sat smoking a lonely pipe, when the 'phone bell rang. I took up the receiver. I think I knew who had called me, even before I heard her voice.

"Is that you, Mr. Decies?"

"Yes, Nanette."

"I am so miserable, because——"

She hesitated.

"Because of what?" I prompted gently.

"Because I never gave you a chance to explain. Oh, Mr. Decies! Tell me—*is* there something I don't know?"

"Why, yes—there is," I replied. "You don't know that Major O'Shea and I were totally ignorant of the plot to trap the man you call Captain Slattery."

"Oh!" came, as a sort of sigh, broken by a sob. "And I told him—— Mr. Decies, do you think you can ever forgive me?"

"I *do* forgive you, Nanette."

"And do you think—— Good-night!"

"Nanette!" I called. "Nanette!" But there was no answer.

CHAPTER XXIV
PETER PAN

A DELICIOUS HAZE HUNG over the Serpentine, by which token I knew that a warm day might be expected. Votaries of Peter Pan were few, for the morning was young as yet, but I sat watching him in his green temple and I thought how puzzled some archæologist of the future was going to be.

Strange to reflect that a Scotsman should add to the ranks of the gods; stranger still that his immortal child should find himself so completely at home upon Olympus. More and more strange the reflection that none of the older gods were jealous.

Children of course came to pay tribute, and I think it was this morning I learned for the first time that there are many juvenile citizens whose day is incomplete unless they have made offering—a laugh, a pointed finger, a fleeting glance—to the god of that dear world which is hidden from most of us behind the gates of innocence. To many an exile under palm and pine, the coming of spring means dreams of crocuses and Peter Pan in Kensington Gardens.

I was suffering from a fit of physical and mental restlessness. I could not clear my mind of the idea that some imminent peril threatened O'Shea. That Nanette was involved, I feared, but tried hard not to believe. Experience of that Red organization known as the S Group had shown its members to be frankly unscrupulous; and Nanette had blindly involved herself with one of them. I knew why she had done it, but the man, Adolf Zara, could not know. For Nanette, Zara had ceased to exist. I doubted that the reverse was true.

The peace of the morning and the beauty of the lake mocked me. In the long encounter between O'Shea and the S Group, honours had gone to the enemy. But the battle was not yet over. Instinct and common sense alike told me that the worst was yet to come.

My ceaseless meditations along these lines had earned me a sleepless night, and I think I had sought out this spot beside the Serpentine with some vague idea of finding peace.

Now, coming out of a brown study and looking up, I observed a figure approaching along the path. It was that of a girl very simply dressed in a gray walking suit, and wearing a tight-fitting hat, which I should have described as claret-coloured but for which the fashion journals no doubt have a better name. Her fingers listlessly interlocked, she came slowly along, looking down at the path and sometimes kicking a pebble aside. Never once did she look up, not even when she arrived before Peter Pan, until:

"Good-morning, Nanette!" said I.

Then she stopped as suddenly as though a physical obstacle had checked her.

"Good heavens!" she replied, tore herself from a land of dreams and stared at me, smiling. But her smile was not exactly a happy one. "It's like a musical comedy, isn't it?"

"Why?" I asked.

"Well, everybody turning up at the same place for no reason!"

"Not everybody," said I.

"Well—no." Nanette hesitated, and then sat down beside me on the bench. "Not everybody."

"Curiously enough," I went on, "I was thinking about you."

Nanette stared at the point of her shoe.

"Must be telepathy," she murmured.

"Why? Were you thinking about me?"

"Yes." She nodded. "I shall never forgive myself for what I have done."

"You mean—about Adolf Zara?"

"About Captain Slattery, yes." She turned to me. "You see, I always think of him as 'Slattery.'"

"Does that make you like him any better, Nanette?"

"No," she admitted; "I have never liked him. But, well—you know how I felt about him? Does Major O'Shea know that I know?"

"You mean," I suggested, "does he know that you no longer suspect him of using you as a lure?"

Nanette nodded without looking up.

"I have had no opportunity of telling him," said I. "But I expect to see him to-day." I rested my hand upon hers, which lay listlessly on the seat beside her. "May I talk to you quite honestly?"

"Of course," said Nanette, but still did not look up.

"I want to tell you," I went on, "that the man you call Captain Slattery, but whose real name is Adolf Zara, is not as civilized as he appears to be. He is a member of a very dangerous organization. I hope you will make a point of avoiding him."

"I am never going to see him again," Nanette declared.

She spoke abstractedly, and it dawned upon me that her interest was centred less upon this matter of her perilous acquaintance with a member of the S Group than upon the passers-by. I attached little significance to the fact at the time, and:

"I am only anxious about your personal safety," I said. "Anything you care to tell me, I shall keep to myself. Are you sure that Captain Slattery does not mean to see *you* again?"

Nanette looked aside at me.

I thought that, since Adolf Zara was human, my question had been rather superfluous. O'Shea, who was no alarmist, had admitted that the secret organization of these people was extensive and efficient. Wild ideas assailed my mind, but:

"Of course, we are no longer in the lonely island of Madeira," I went on, "but in the capital of a civilized country. All the same, Nanette, I should be glad to know that Zara was no longer in England."

"So should I," she admitted, and looked away again.

The words were simple enough, but, from what I knew of Nanette, I detected an unfamiliar note in her voice. I was not sorry to hear it, although it was a note of fear. It told me that my warning had been unnecessary. Nanette knew that Zara was a dangerous man.

"I have been wondering what I should do," she began suddenly. "But now I have made up my mind."

She opened her handbag and took out a twisted scrap of paper. Smoothing it carefully, she passed it to me, and:

"Captain Slattery dropped this yesterday," she said, "while he was with me in a taxi. I think, perhaps——"

She hesitated.

"Yes?" said I, glancing at what was written on the paper.

"It's so odd that I think, perhaps, you should show it to—your friend."

Watching her as she spoke, I wondered at the scheme of things; wondered whether she would outlive a romance born in a jewelled island, or whether, despite her youth, it was real, for good or ill, this love of hers for O'Shea.

I suppressed a sigh, and bent over the writing. This was what I read:

Book from Charing Cross to the British Museum. From the Mansion House also it is no distance to the British Museum. Hyde Park there is a station. Change at Charing Cross for Piccadilly. Bond Street is merely Bond Street, and two London Bridges are better than one Bond Street. But the Mansion House and the British Museum are national institutions, and Berkeley

Square pulled down or Berkeley Square blown up would only lead to the Old Bailey. Residents at the Crystal Palace rarely moved to Berkeley Square, and the Tower Bridge is new whilst London Bridge is old. Meet you in Bond Street.

I raised my eyes. Nanette was stifling laughter. Now she stifled it no longer. And Nanette's laughter was very sweet music.

"Of course," she confessed, "I know it *seems* perfectly idiotic! But one never knows. It may mean a general strike or something. But whatever it means, I shall have to be pushing along. I am meeting Mumsy at Marshall's."

She stood up, looking sharply to right and left, and I wondered what this might portend. However, we took the path to the Gate, walking very slowly, and from there proceeded in a taxi.

I dropped Nanette at her destination and was standing outside the shop wondering whether to walk over to the Club or to hunt up O'Shea, when an explanation of this chance meeting presented itself.

O'Shea, I recalled, had once said, in Nanette's presence, that when he had a difficult problem upon his mind, he varied the ordinary routine of a London morning. Other duties permitting, he walked as far as Peter Pan, and in the presence of the little god not infrequently discovered a solution of his difficulties.

Nanette had been unfortunate. This morning O'Shea had not come.

I reëntered the taxi which I had kept waiting, and:

"Lancaster Gate," I directed.

Why I did so I have no idea; but experience has taught me that the motives which prompt many far-reaching actions are so obscure as to defy subsequent research.

Discharging the man, I set out along that path beside the Serpentine. The hour was now approaching noon, and platoons of white-capped nursemaids promenaded with the younger generation. I found myself surrounded by future society beauties; statesmen who would be making laws when I was an old man; great soldiers destined to save the British Empire from enemies yet unborn; actresses whose reputations might overshadow the memory of Sarah Bernhardt; princesses, dukes, vagabonds, thieves; some in perambulators, others in miniature automobiles, some toddling; a fascinating crowd.

Then I awakened from my day dream. Standing squarely in front of Peter Pan, and watching that youthful deity with a fixed stare, was O'Shea! He remained unaware of my presence until I touched him on the shoulder.

He turned swiftly. And I saw a far-away look in his gray eyes instantly change to one of close scrutiny; then:

"Decies," he said, "I am glad to see you. I learned something last night."

"What?" I said.

"I learned why Adolf Zara has come to England! The president of the S Group—a person with the mentality of a Tomsky and the morals of a baboon—is one Schmidt."

"Well?" said I.

"Schmidt is in London!"

CHAPTER XXV
THE SECOND MESSAGE

"Of course," I said, "it may mean nothing."

O'Shea raised his eyes from the extraordinary communication that I had handed to him, and:

"Or it may mean everything!" he added.

We sat on that bench by the water's edge where I had met Nanette. O'Shea continued his scrutiny of the message, and, looking over his shoulder, I read it again for perhaps the twentieth time. Its absurdity fogged me. Passers-by ceased to exist, and I forgot Peter Pan.

"Perhaps," said I, "it is some kind of code."

"Since it is otherwise meaningless," O'Shea murmured, without raising his eyes, "your suggestion is excellent. You will have noticed that there are three references to the British Museum and that the expression 'Two London Bridges' occurs?"

"I had not particularly noticed this," I admitted.

"Two London Bridges," O'Shea went on musingly. "Very interesting—very interesting. You see where I mean?"

He indicated the passage with the rim of his monocle.

"Quite," said I eagerly. "But Charing Cross, Berkeley Square, and Bond Street also occur several times."

"But only Bond Street and Berkeley Square crop up in pairs," he replied, "if we exclude the brace of London Bridges."

And now, as we sat there pondering over this nonsensical piece of writing, came a strange interruption.

"Have you seen Comrade Zara?" said a guttural voice.

I looked up sharply. A stout German obstructed my view of Kensington Gardens. His ample face was draped in a pleasant smile, and he surveyed O'Shea and myself through a pair of spectacles that resembled portholes. No doubt I was gaping like an imbecile but O'Shea rose to the situation lightly.

"He is here," he replied calmly. "Are you from Comrade Schmidt?"

"I am," said the German. His smile disappeared. Relieved of it, his face was frankly sinister. "Have you seen Comrade Wilson?"

Perhaps it is unnecessary to state that emerging from a perusal of the letter about Hyde Park, Bond Street, and Berkeley Square, and finding myself plunged into this apparently inane conversation, I began to doubt my own sanity; but:

"*This* is Comrade Wilson," said O'Shea gravely, and waved his hand in my direction!

The German nodded in a very brusque way.

"Show me the order," he demanded.

O'Shea held up the demented document we had been reading; whereupon:

"Good," said our eccentric acquaintance. "Quick! The order for to-night!" He passed an envelope to O'Shea. "I am followed. Good-morning."

He moved off hurriedly, and I was still staring in speechless astonishment when a thick-set man wearing a blue suit and a soft hat, and who, without resembling a straggler from the Row, might have been a Colonial visitor, came along the path. One keen side-glance he gave us, and then disappeared in the wake of our Teutonic acquaintance.

"O'Shea——" I began; but:

"After all," he interrupted me, "one must admit that the Scotland Yard people are efficient. That was a detective-inspector of the Special Branch."

"Do you mean he is following the German?"

"Undoubtedly."

"But why should he follow him? Who was the German?"

"I haven't the faintest idea!" O'Shea replied.

"But he mentioned Zara! And you seemed to know him."

O'Shea adjusted his monocle and looked me over in a way that I didn't like.

"Really, Decies," he replied, "considering the admirable assistance which you have given me in this matter—for which I shall always be grateful—there are times when you defeat me. Why our German friend reposed his confidence in us I have no more idea than the Man in the Moon, nor why he confided this letter to my keeping. But his reference to Zara brands him a member of the S Group, without the significant fact that he is being followed by an officer of the Special Branch, whom I chance to know but who does not know me. The weary arm of coincidence is not long enough to embrace all these happenings, Decies. There is some other explanation. Let us see if it is here."

He tore open the envelope and withdrew a single sheet of paper. I bent forward eagerly, and over his shoulder read the following:

Charing Cross, London Bridge, Hyde Park, and the Strand are
all worthy of a visit. Kingsway is modern, but the British Mu-

seum, Tower Bridge, the Mansion House, especially the British Museum, must not be neglected. Hyde Park merits several visits. The Mansion House, or the British Museum, can be done in one day, but Hyde Park is the only Hyde Park, whilst Piccadilly and the Strand are merely thoroughfares. The British Museum exhibit 365A is not in the National Gallery. The Crystal Palace does not resemble Buckingham Palace and Bond Street is not the Station for the Crystal Palace. Shepherd's Market is a survival. But book at Kingsway. Meet you at the Mansion House.

"And now," said O'Shea, "you know as much as I do!"

I stared at him blankly, and, as I stared, heard clocks, near and remote, strike the hour of noon. O'Shea suddenly thrust the second letter into his pocket and began to study that which Nanette had given to me.

He looked up, staring intently at the figure of Peter Pan, then:

"Twelve o'clock," he muttered. "Does the fact that it is twelve o'clock convey anything to you, Decies?"

"Nothing," I confessed, "except that I feel thirsty."

But it had conveyed something more to O'Shea. A distinguished officer is not relieved of his ordinary duties and dispatched to the Argentine upon the toss of a coin. He is selected for his special qualifications. That O'Shea's qualifications were extensive I had already learned; that they were also peculiar was beginning to dawn upon me.

CHAPTER XXVI
THE CRYPTOGRAM

NANETTE WAS WITH A party at the Hippodrome that night, and I had promised to look in during the interval. The curtain had just fallen and the orchestra was playing as I entered with O'Shea. The manager met us at the top of the steps.

No doubt you remember him. He is unforgettable, being the best-dressed manager in Europe. He was delighted to meet O'Shea and much happier in greeting an officer of the Household troops who had come in for a drink than in endorsing a plebeian check for the use of the Royal box.

Nanette came running out ahead of her party and stopped dead on seeing O'Shea. He bowed in his grave, courtly fashion. She glanced at me swiftly, and then:

"Oh, Major O'Shea," she said, "I want to ask you to forgive me!"

"And I want to thank you," said he.

"To thank me?"

Nanette looked up at him and then down again very swiftly. She began tapping her foot upon the rubber-coated floor.

"To thank you," he repeated, "once more. It seems to be my happy fate, Nanette, to be always thanking you."

"But what have you to thank me for?" she asked, industriously studying the point of her shoe.

"For giving me an opportunity of redeeming my many failures."

Nanette looked up—she was quite calm again—and met his eyes bravely.

"Some of them," she said, "have been my fault."

"You are wrong," O'Shea assured her. "The fault has been mine from the very beginning."

"What do you mean?" she asked; and I turned aside, joining some friends who had just come out from the stalls.

In spite of my determination about Nanette, it still hurt a little bit to see that light in her eyes.

"I mean," I heard O'Shea reply, "that I have tried to do something that is impossible."

I heard no more, nor did I want to.

That bell which indicates the rise of the curtain releases from the bars of a London theatre certain characteristic types. The wet man returning guiltily with guarded breath to his dry wife in the stalls, having stepped out to "smoke a cigarette." The bored man, who is present under protest, and who goes to his seat like a martyr to the stake. The victim of jazzitis who dances with his girl friend in the lobby, and post-mortem examination of whose skull reveals the presence of several perfectly formed saxophones but nothing else.

The curtain was about to rise and practically everybody was seated when I learned that Nanette had straggled. She stood with O'Shea in the opening at the back of the stalls. And I thought that I had never before seen her so animated in his company.

Envied model of her girl friends, Nanette was a paragon of self-possession in the company of all men, or had been until she had met O'Shea. Never, hitherto, had I seen her at her ease with him. But to-night she was—realized that she was—and her happy excitement will be good to remember when I am ten years older.

One hand resting upon his arm, she looked up, talking gaily. He, too, had relaxed, as any man must have done finding himself in the company of an adorably pretty and spirited girl who loved him so much that she didn't care who knew. He was laughing like a schoolboy.

The curtain was up before Nanette tore herself away. She was very flushed, and I know her heart was beating wildly. I pitied her escort, foreseeing that she would be abstracted throughout the remainder of the evening.

O'Shea turned to me, and his eyes were still glistening happily.

"Well, Decies," said he, "what are you thinking?"

"I am thinking," I replied honestly, "that we are about of an age. That if Nanette had looked at me as I saw her looking at you, I should have asked her to marry me before I let her go back to her seat."

He stared very hard, his expression changing from second to second; then:

"Being Celtic," he said, "I suppose I am superstitious. At every turn since I have met her Nanette has intruded in my life. I am beginning to wonder."

"About what are you thinking in particular?" I asked.

"About the letter that Zara dropped in the cab and that Nanette gave to you."

"Have you fathomed it?" I asked excitedly—"and the other?"

"Both are in the same code. But without the first I doubt that I should have been able to read the second."

"Then you *have* read them?"

"I have," O'Shea replied; "and this time Nanette has dealt me a full hand."

His suppressed excitement communicated itself to me.

"What have you learned?" I said eagerly. "Can I be of any assistance?"

"Your assistance is indispensable!" he returned. "Are you game?"

"Every time!"

"Good enough. Let us go along to your rooms, and I will explain what to-night has in store for us."

As the taxi that we presently hailed threaded its way through the traffic of Cranbourne Street, and on through that of Piccadilly, I glanced aside several times at my silent companion. I wondered if his abstraction might be ascribed to the problem of the S Group, or to that of Nanette. Not being an O'Shea, I hesitated to judge. But my vote was for Nanette.

Arrived at my rooms and having sampled the whisky and soda:

"Now," O'Shea began, "the mantle of Edgar Allan Poe not having fallen upon my shoulders, I doubt that I should have solved this cipher but for the happy coincidence of meeting our German friend in the very shadow of Peter Pan. You will recall, too, that at the moment of his departure, the clocks were chiming the hour of noon."

"I remember," said I.

"I turned it over in my mind, considering the thing from every conceivable angle. Before I tackled the cipher—for of course the messages were palpably written in some kind of cipher—one fact was plain enough to me."

"What was that?"

"The fact that Zara, an important member of the S Group, was not known by sight to the member who spoke to us! He mistook *me* for Zara, and he mistook *you* for one Comrade Wilson, of whom I had never heard, and respecting whom I have no instructions."

"So far I agree," said I, "but what I simply cannot make out is why this deranged German should walk up to two perfect strangers seated in Kensington Gardens and take it for granted that they were the people he was looking for."

"His opening remark was non-committal," O'Shea reminded me, reflectively sipping his whisky and soda.

"Certainly it was; but am I to assume that the man was walking about London addressing the inquiry, 'Have you seen Comrade Zara?' to every male citizen he met on his travels?"

"The very point that led me to a solution of the problem," O'Shea returned. "I realized, of course, that the routine which you indicate would have been insane, and I do not look for insanity of this kind from members of the S Group. I recalled that we had been sitting by the statue of Peter Pan, and that I had drawn your attention to the presence of 'Two London Bridges' in the message. I noted that the double bridges were preceded by a reference to

Bond Street—or, rather, by two references to Bond Street—and followed by another. I remembered that the hour was noon.

"Treating the message as a cipher, I assumed, as a basis of investigation, that the various well-known spots mentioned represented letters and that all intervening words might be neglected. Now, I had two almost certain clues to work upon.

"First, that our German friend clearly expected to meet Zara and someone called Wilson by the statue of Peter Pan. Second, that he expected to meet them there at noon. Think for a moment, and you will realize that this must have been the case."

"It is clear enough," said I, "now that you point it out to me."

"His handing me a second message in the same cipher," O'Shea went on, "suggested that the first related to the appointment which we, by bounty of the gods, had accidentally kept. I therefore assumed that the first message conveyed something of this sort: 'Be at the statue of Peter Pan at midday.'

"I began to examine it with this idea in mind. Particularly, I was looking for a sequence to fit the name, Peter Pan. As you can see—" he spread the original messages on my table before me—"it appears unmistakably at the very beginning. Charing Cross is the first point mentioned; four other London landmarks occur, and then Charing Cross again. I assumed as a working theory that Charing Cross stood for the letter P.

"This suggested that British Museum was E as it occurs next, is followed by Mansion House, and then occurs again.

"Assuming Mansion House to be T, we get P-e-t-e. Calling Hyde Park R, we get Peter. Charing Cross then crops up in its correct place. Reading Piccadilly as A and Bond Street as N gives Peter Pan."

He laid his cigarette in an ash-tray and bent over the writing enthusiastically.

"This enabled me to cross-check, for Bond Street occurs again immediately, with the two London Bridges which first attracted my attention, followed by another Bond Street.

"Bond Street being N, it was reasonable to assume that London Bridge was O, making—Peter Pan, Noon."

"By gad!" I exclaimed. "It's wonderful!"

"On the contrary," O'Shea assured me, "it is elementary. To continue: we now have Mansion House again, or T, followed by British Museum—E, and two Berkeley Squares, hitherto unmentioned. Old Bailey and Crystal Palace crop up next—very defeating—followed by a third Berkeley Square. Then Tower Bridge. This is followed by London Bridge, O, and Bond Street, N. Remembering the name of the Comrade for whom you were mistaken, Decies,

I very quickly determined that Berkeley Square stood for L and the word
following 'Noon' was 'Tell.' This gave me a pair of blanks, then L, another
blank, and o-n. Wilson was clearly indicated, and I had my complete message.
'Peter Pan noon, tell Wilson.' "

O'Shea replaced his cigarette between his lips and turned to me, smiling.

"You mean," said I, "that you have read the second message?"

"Naturally," he replied. "It is childishly easy, once having got the idea of the
nature of the cipher. Without bothering you with details, such as the letters
implied by Buckingham Palace, Shepherd's Market, and Kingsway—places
that don't occur in the first message—I may say that it reads as follows: 'Porchester Terrace 365A—which I assume to be the number of a
house—midnight.' "

"Good heavens!" I glanced at the clock. "And he said the order was for
to-night!"

"To-night," O'Shea returned, glancing up. "We have two hours."

"We have two hours?"

"Precisely," said he, and his gray eyes surveyed me unblinkingly. "There are
certain chances, but there is no game without chances, and we shall be covered by a raid squad from Scotland Yard. Whether Comrade Schmidt is more
familiar with the appearance of Comrades Zara and Wilson than his emissary
seems to be, I cannot say. But to-night at twelve o'clock I suggest that you and
I present ourselves at number 365A Porchester Terrace, as Comrades Zara and
Wilson! It is asking a lot, Decies, but are you game?"

"Good God!" I said, hesitated for one electric moment, and then held out
my hand.

O'Shea grasped it.

CHAPTER XXVII
THE COMRADES GATHER

"Nanette has gone on somewhere to dance," said O'Shea.

"I know." I stared out of the window of the taxi. "I take it that she doesn't know where *we* have gone on to?"

"No."

O'Shea's reply was little more than a whisper, but it told me that which made me at once glad and sorry. For good or for ill, Nanette was winning.

"Two things are rather worrying me," O'Shea confessed. "It is obvious enough that Zara is afraid to visit any of the known centres of the S Group, hence the appointment at Peter Pan. He probably received the letter—or 'Order'—at some post office, under an assumed name. But if he had read it and decoded it before he dropped it in the taxi, where was he at noon to-day?"

"Unable to approach Peter Pan," I replied promptly, "because we were there, not to mention the man from Scotland Yard who was following the German."

"Yes," O'Shea mused. "Zara's reaction to this check is one of the points I am wondering about. It may prove to be a snag. The second snag——"

But as our taxi had turned into Porchester Terrace and was now pulling up, I did not learn what the second snag might be.

We alighted, and I looked up and down the street. Save for O'Shea's assurance, there was nothing to show that our movements were covered by the squad from Scotland Yard. Porchester Terrace proclaimed itself empty from end to end, or for as far as I could see.

Number 365A was a prosperous-looking mansion set back beyond a patch of shrubbery and approached through a sort of arcade guarded by handsome double doors. What appeared to be a large room on the first floor was brilliantly lighted, but otherwise the house was in darkness.

"Pull over to the other side of the street," O'Shea directed the taxi driver, "and wait. We shall not be long."

"Very good, sir."

As the man turned his cab:

"Now," said O'Shea, "we are going over the top! Are you fit?"

"All ready," said I.

O'Shea pressed the bell button.

In the interval that elapsed between the ringing of the bell and the opening of the door, I conjured up a picture of Nanette dancing with somebody or another somewhere, perpetually glancing abstractedly about the room, as I had seen her do so often, in hope of catching a glimpse of O'Shea.

It was hard to believe that this doorway before which we waited represented a frontier which, once crossed, shut us off from the life of empty gaiety which the name of London conveys to so many; difficult to regard it as the porch of a grim and real underworld, controlled by enemies of established society, remorseless, almost inhuman in their bloodthirsty fanaticism.

A saturnine foreign butler admitted us. We had shed our dinner kit and were wearing tweeds.

"Comrade Zara and Comrade Wilson," said O'Shea with composure.

The man nodded and stood aside. We entered the arcade, which was bordered by plants in pots, and saw ahead of us some carpeted steps, lighted by a hanging lantern.

As the double doors closed behind us, I experienced one of those indescribable moments compounded of panic and exhilaration. Then somewhere, very dimly, I heard a clock striking midnight. We were going upstairs.

"Comrade Zara and Comrade Wilson."

I found myself in a large room, very simply furnished in library fashion, and in the presence of six or seven rather unsavoury human specimens, some of whom bowed curtly, and some of whom did not bow at all.

Our Peter Pan acquaintance was present; and a short thick-set man, who had incredibly long arms, and who generally resembled a red baboon, came forward to greet us. He had incomplete teeth, and those that survived badly needed scaling. His accent opened up wide possibilities.

"Greeting, Comrades," said he. "You are welcome. My name is Schmidt."

And as he spoke, fixing his piercing glance first upon O'Shea and then upon myself, I recognized beneath that uncouth exterior the primitive, formidable force of the man.

He presented the other comrades, by names which are not to be found in Debrett, and I reflected that impudence is indispensable to success in this sort of game.

It became evident that, from Comrade Schmidt downward, nobody in the room was familiar with the appearance of either Zara or Wilson!

An appalling-looking bearded creature attached itself to O'Shea.

"We are anxious, Comrade," it said, "to hear your personal account of the state of the work in South Africa."

"I am not too hopeful," O'Shea replied gloomily, and glanced aside at me.

"But," said Schmidt, turning his dreadful little eyes in my direction, "Comrade Wilson brings us news from the United States which will be like new blood in our veins."

Somehow or another, O'Shea managed to shake off the Missing Link, and to secure a word aside with me.

"Very full bag," he murmured. "If we make no mistakes, we shall purge England and America of some unsavoury elements. But the second snag which I had foreseen rests on the fact that another steamer from Madeira has reached Southampton since we returned. There is one member of the S Group whom we left behind. He knows us both. He might quite conceivably have been in that steamer! His appearance here would raise the temperature considerably. And——"

He was interrupted. The door of the room was thrown open and the foreign butler entered.

"Comrade Macalister," he announced.

"The snag to which I referred!" said O'Shea.

CHAPTER XXVIII
THE RAID

I SUPPOSE THAT AT some time during his life every man who has anything of the boy left in him has thought that he would like to take a fling at the great adventure of Secret Service. I feel called upon to assure these aspirants that a comfortable armchair is the better choice.

Accident, or that Higher Power which the Arabs call Kismet, had cast me into the path of Edmond O'Shea. He had honoured me with his friendship, but had quite failed to recognize that I was a man of lesser stature than his own. Whilst granting every honour to marshal and statesman, personally I am disposed to believe that it was men such as O'Shea who steered the Allies to victory; and perhaps, hitherto, I had been inclined to look upon the Secret Service as a job for highbrows rather than for soldiers.

This error was to be corrected.

Conceive a large room filled with enemies of established order; fanatics, whose collected scruples would have left a thimble empty. Conceive that I and O'Shea, posing as members of their bloodthirsty organization, were amongst them as spies, pledged to bring about their ruin.

Now, conceive that a "Comrade," who knows us and has fared ill at our hands, is suddenly announced.

Perhaps I shall be forgiven when I say that I remembered with gratitude how Edmond O'Shea had rallied a company of the Guards during the great retreat, how his presence of mind and consummate self-possession had helped historians to chronicle Cambrai with pride rather than with humility.

He edged up beside me. I saw him fumbling for his monocle and saw his change of expression when he realized that he had left it behind; then:

"Get near the door," he murmured. "My fault, Decies, to have let you in for this. But I had hoped to learn things that police examination can never bring out."

Macalister came in.

He was in dinner kit and he smoked a cigar which, to my disordered vision, appeared to be decorated with two bands. His superb self-possession was worthy of Tom Mix. He did not merely own the room; he possessed the property.

"Take the left," said O'Shea.

Unerringly, instinctively, Macalister's glance settled upon us at the moment of his entrance. He had advanced no more than one pace beyond the butler, and his mouth was agape for excited utterance, when O'Shea's revolver had him covered.

Overwhelmed with a sense of utter unreality, I covered the group of four on my left which included the formidable Schmidt.

Glibly, as though born of long familiarity, the words leapt to my tongue: "Hands up!"

The command was obeyed. And I have since thought, paradoxical though it may appear, that violent men, in these matters, are more tractable than men of peace. Assessing human life lightly, they credit the brain behind the gun with compunction no greater than their own.

"By God!" I heard Macalister say—and I hope I shall always find time to take off my hat to a good loser—"I had you wrong all along, Major!"

Schmidt looked dangerously ugly for a moment; then:

"Line up," said O'Shea sharply. "Jump to it. Fall in on the left of Schmidt."

Came inarticulate mutterings, but without other audible protest the group obeyed, forming a line having Schmidt at one end and the saturnine butler at the other.

"Now," O'Shea continued, "if any man lowers his hands, I shall not argue with him. Decies, will you go down to the street door and whistle? Pass behind me. Keep a sharp look-out. I don't know who is in the house."

I obeyed, the sense of unreality prevailing. But I know I shall always remember that row of sullen-faced men with raised hands, who watched as I crossed behind O'Shea.

There was no one on the stairs, and no one in the long, glazed passage that led to the street. This gained, I ran the length of it, and throwing open the double doors beheld a seemingly deserted Porchester Terrace.

I whistled shrilly. The result was magical.

Springing from what hiding places I know not, men appeared running from right and left! This was the raid squad from Scotland Yard, and I realized that I was helping to mould history.

Our taximan, who was waiting on the other side of the street, and who had been peacefully smoking a cigarette, jumped down from his seat and watched the proceedings with an expression of stupefaction that was comic in its intensity.

Everything was carried out in a most orderly manner. The members of the Group were arrested without unnecessary fuss. The whole thing might have been "produced" by David Belasco. A six-seater car appeared from somewhere or another, in which the gang was canned as neatly as tinned sardines.

The police handled the job with such discretion that chance passers-by never dreamed that anything unusual was going forward. They do these raids much better on the screen.

Macalister was the last to come down from above, his cigar still held firmly between his teeth. He was unperturbed. Deportation was the worst he had to fear, and he knew it quite well. He was smiling slyly. He paused, looking hard at O'Shea and at myself.

"Listen," he said, "you two boys have doubled on me pretty badly, but I don't bear no malice." His grammar at times revealed the influence of the Cubist school. "Zara is different, and he's still loose. Take my tip and watch out for Zara. If he's seeing red, don't try to pet him. Good-night!"

He entered the car, urged by two detectives.

"Good-night," murmured O'Shea thoughtfully, and turned to me.

"You know, Decies," he went on, "if that man had had our advantages, he would have made a damned good sportsman."

There were certain formalities to be attended to, and I suppose it was close upon two o'clock when O'Shea and I found ourselves outside my rooms. I suggested a doch-an'-dorris.

"If I were superstitious," O'Shea declared, "I should refuse."

He smiled, glancing up at the tall ladder beneath which we must walk to reach my door.

"Oh!" said I, "they are mending the roof, or something."

"I suppose we might risk it," he replied; and we went in.

The incident stuck in my mind, not so much because of any superstitious significance that I attached to it as because of what actually happened later.

O'Shea dropped on to the settee in my big room and sighed rather wearily as he watched me preparing drinks.

"You know, Decies," said he, "I am both glad and sorry that this job is over. I have blundered through by sheer good luck. Without your aid, and the aid of someone else, I should have crashed badly."

"Perhaps not," I returned. "If you had not succeeded in one way, you might quite easily have found another."

"Or I might not," said he. "No. I am a poor policeman, and peace-time soldiering is no sort of game."

"What do you mean, O'Shea?"

"I mean," he replied, holding up to the light a glass that I had handed to him, "that I am infernally restless."

I sighed as loudly as he had done and stooped over the syphon. Then:

"Decies," said O'Shea, "we live in a generation that grows up very early."

"We do," I agreed.

"I should like to talk to you seriously. There are many men I have known longer, but none I could sooner trust. Yet in this matter somehow I don't feel..."

"Yes?" I prompted.

"Well, I don't feel quite at liberty to discuss it with you."

There was a silence that might have been awkward. O'Shea was watching me almost pathetically; and:

"I know what you want to talk about," I said. "Nanette is a witch. But there is only one man in the world for her now. It might be fair, though, to give her a year to think it over."

"You don't doubt *my* attitude in the matter," O'Shea murmured.

"No," I replied, "I know it."

He looked at me very fixedly, when:

"Coo-ooh!" I heard.

O'Shea's expression changed; and, turning, I crossed to an open window, looking down into the street.

Standing just in front of the ladder which disfigured the front of the premises, was Nanette, staring upward. A two-seater with several people in it stood at the curb.

"Hello, Nanette," I called.

"Saw your light," she shouted, "as we were passing. May we come up, or are you going to bed?"

"No," I replied, and hesitated to tell her what I knew she hoped. "Come right up and bring your friends. I have only just got in."

"Right-oh!" she cried.

CHAPTER XXIX
ADOLPH ZARA

THE PARTY THAT PRESENTLY invaded us proved to consist of Nanette and a brunette girl friend whom I had not seen before. They were escorted by a young medical officer on leave from Mesopotamia—a very charming type of Scotsman—and Milton, one of Nanette's Madeira conquests, whom, you may recall, I had met again recently under rather odd circumstances. I thought that this evening was probably his reward for the weary job of scouting that he had performed on that occasion.

He was not a happy man. The fact was beginning to dawn upon him that at the Savoy, the Hippodrome, and wherever else they had gone, he had been wasting his fragrance on the desert air. I pictured him driving to my apartment as one consciously heading for his doom.

The poor fellow was rather pathetically young, and, regarding every acquaintance of Nanette's as a serious rival, he had awakened to the fact that he had three score or so of deadly enemies in London. Presently:

"Whisky and soda?" said I; "or have you reached the Bass stage?"

"Neither, thanks," he returned, and glared around my modest bachelor apartment as one who finds himself in the chamber of Bluebeard.

Nanette had sped to O'Shea like an arrow to its target. As I turned aside from the peevish Milton, "I hadn't dared to hope I should see you again to-night," I heard her say.

The other man and the pretty brunette were jointly occupying my most comfortable armchair, therefore, conquering a perfectly stupid pique which Milton had inspired:

"Well," said I, holding out my cigarette case, "we seem to have no alternative but to—look on, Milton."

He rejected the olive-branch, and, rudely ignoring my proffered case, crossed to the settee where Nanette and O'Shea sat side by side.

"I say, Nanette," he exclaimed, "what about going on to Chelsea?"

Nanette barely glanced up as she replied:

"No, I don't want to dance any more to-night, Jim."

"Why not dance here?" cried her friend, pointing in the direction of the piano. "Do you play, Mr. Decies?"

"Not dance music," I confessed gladly.

"But Jim does," she went on. "Go on, Jim! Just one."

"Jim" crossed to the piano, offering an excellent imitation of an ox approaching Chicago. He crashed into a piece of syncopation that put years on the instrument. I had never heard the item before and trust that I shall never hear it again. I saw O'Shea smilingly shake his head; then Nanette ran across to me, and off we went around the furniture, I wondering which would burst first, a wire in my reeling piano or a blood-vessel in the empurpled skull of the player.

Nanette danced because she was too happy to keep still, even with O'Shea beside her. I danced because I had no choice in the matter. It was an odd business, pointedly illustrating the part that Terpsichore plays in this modern civilization of ours.

Nanette was dancing with me, but she wanted to dance with O'Shea. The other pair didn't want to dance at all. They just wanted to be alone together. And Milton didn't want to be the band. In fact, the whole thing was a sort of neutral territory, or sanctuary, in which the various protagonists found temporary refuge.

I don't know what momentous decision Nanette's girl friend was shirking, but when Milton threatened to weaken:

"Go on, Jim! Please go on!" she cried, avoiding the ardent gaze of her partner.

Milton, the most ferociously reluctant musician I have ever seen at work, made a renewed assault upon the keyboard. He was watching Nanette, who rarely took her eyes off O'Shea; and a vein rose unpleasantly upon his forehead. He perpetrated some discords that set my teeth on edge.

How long this might have continued I hesitate to guess. Milton's gorge was rising tropically. I doubt that his destruction of my piano would have ceased while life remained in the instrument, but an interruption came.

Nanette and I had navigated an awkward channel behind the armchair and were beating up toward the settee and O'Shea. The man from Mesopotamia had ingeniously steered his partner into a little book-lined recess at the farther end of the room. I had my back to the open window and Nanette was facing it. Suddenly she grew rigid.

Her face became transfigured with an expression of horror that I can never forget. She pulled up dead—staring, staring past me, into the darkness of the street beyond.

"What is it, Nanette?" I began, when the music ceased with a crash and I saw Milton bound to his feet.

Unconsciously, I had gripped Nanette hard. But, in the next instant, she wrenched herself free from my grasp, turned, and with a queer sort of smothered cry threw herself upon O'Shea!

I twisted about.

Not two feet behind me an arm protruded into the room! The hand grasped a strange-looking pistol—for at that time I had never seen a Maxim Silencer. I heard a muffled thud. Something came whizzing through the air in my direction. (I learned later, when clarity came, that it was a valuable Ming vase that had stood upon the piano.)

"Hold him, Decies!" yelled Milton.

It was Milton who had hurled this costly projectile at the dimly seen arm in the window. The vase went crashing out into the street. I heard a second thud. Milton fell forward across the instrument—and then slid down on to the carpet. The hand clutching the pistol had vanished.

A sort of vague red mist was dancing before my eyes. Came a rush of footsteps. Nanette was slipping from O'Shea's arms. His face as he looked down into hers was a mask of tragedy. I heard her utter a little moan and I saw a streak of blood upon one white shoulder.

Then followed chaos.

A very weak voice, which vaguely I recognized as that of Milton, said:

"Don't worry about me, Doc. Look after Nanette."

I saw O'Shea stoop and lift Nanette. I saw her pale face. When, cutting through the tumult like a ray from a beacon:

"The window, Decies! Watch which way he goes!"

Automatically, I obeyed O'Shea. I strained out, looking to right and to left of the ladder. It was boarded over, but I realized that a desperate man, given sufficient agility, could have climbed the rungs from underneath, as evidently the assassin had done.

At first, the street seemed to be empty from end to end; then I saw the figure of a man emerge from shadow into a patch of light cast by a street lamp—one who walked swiftly in the direction of Berkeley Square. I withdrew my head and stared, only half believing, about the room.

Milton, looking deathly, lay propped up against the piano. He met my glance, and:

"Seen him?" he demanded.

I turned, as the military surgeon who had been bending over Nanette looked up at her friend, who stood beside him.

"Know anything about nursing?" he jerked.

The girl was very pale, but:

"Yes," she answered bravely, meeting his eyes, "a little. Tell me what to do, and I will do it."

He nodded, smiling, whereat I was reassured, and then:

"Have you a manservant in the house, Mr. Decies?" he asked.

"Yes."

"Dig him out. I can manage. You fellows are in the way. Get after the swine who did this."

But O'Shea had already started for the door. His expression was one I had rather not have seen. There is a savage hidden in every Celt, if one digs deep through.

The other members of the group by this time were safely housed in cells. I thought that if we were destined to overtake Adolf Zara, he was likely to enjoy the distinction of spending the night in a morgue.

CHAPTER XXX
MEMORIES CAN SAVE

As MILTON'S CAR, DRIVEN by O'Shea, raced around the corner into the square, all question of the fugitive's identity was settled.

Just vaulting into a two-seater that had been parked over by the railings was the man whose retreating figure I had seen as I leaned from the window! I prayed that he might be unable to start. But my prayer was not answered. Off he went, heading for Piccadilly.

One swift glance back he gave over his shoulder. And in the light of the street lamp by which the car had stood, I saw the face of Zara!

I glanced at O'Shea beside me. His pale features were set like a mask. I looked to right and to left; but not a soul was in sight. Berkeley Square was apparently deserted. Often enough I had wondered how certain notorious burglaries had been accomplished with all the resources of civilization at beck and call of justice. This was the answer.

We had no means of arranging for Zara's interception—although a constable was on duty at the corner of Bruton Street! We could only hope to keep him in sight or else overtake him. The merest hitch, or slightest traffic delay, would deliver him into our hands. But the betting was equal. Such an accident might as well befall us as him; and, the quarry once out of sight, our chances fell below zero.

O'Shea spoke never a word. His mind held but one single purpose. That purpose, I firmly believe, was to wreak justice upon Zara with his own hands.

Momentarily, I wondered about Milton. Of Nanette I dared not think. But a cold fury was growing within me, and I fingered the pistol that had been in my pocket since the raid upon the house in Porchester Terrace.

Zara whirled round into St. James's Street. The traffic in Piccadilly was not great but there were a number of pedestrians about. I even saw policemen in the distance. It all seemed utterly grotesque. Then, hot upon the fugitive, we, too, were dropping down the slope. Far ahead I could see the clock above St. James's Palace. The hour was a quarter past two.

Our speed was outrageous. We crossed Pall Mall at about thirty-five, and came out into the Mall, heading for Buckingham Palace in Brooklands fashion. We were gaining slightly. We crept from forty-five to fifty. Broad thoroughfares, brightly lighted, offered no obstruction; and we flew around the sharp bend by the Victoria Memorial and headed east.

"Westminster Bridge!" I muttered.

O'Shea did not speak. Past the barracks we sped, and, undeterred by a certain amount of traffic in Parliament Square, shot on to the approach to the Bridge. We were now three lengths behind Zara, and on the gradient began to improve upon it. Zara drove on the inside of the car lines, hugging the pavement. And at about the centre of the Bridge we passed outside him. I heard someone shouting.

"Cover him, Decies!" said O'Shea grimly. "Shoot if he doesn't pull up!"

I turned and gave a loud cry. Zara had slowed down and was already twenty yards behind us!

"Stop, O'Shea!" I cried—"stop!"

He obeyed so suddenly that I nearly dived through the windshield. Then we jumped, one on either side, and started to run back.

Zara had already dismounted, and I saw him peeling his coat. A picture arose out of the recent past: a foggy night off Ushant: and I seemed to hear again that eerie cry, "Man overboard!"

So it was that Zara had eluded us once before. Undoubtedly he was going to do so again; and for all the cold hatred in my heart, I could not entirely withhold admiration as I saw him bound upon the parapet, raise his arms, and take that appalling dive into the Thames far below.

I knew now, however, what I had not known formerly: that Adolf Zara's courage was the courage of madness. His was that disease of fanaticism which, when it does not cough up a Tomsky, floods the criminal lunatic asylums.

As we both craned over the parapet, peering down at the uneasy water, I heard the sound of a runner and then the flat note of a police whistle.

"There he is!" said O'Shea.

I stared but could see nothing, when:

"Hello, there! What's the game! Who was it that went over?" cried a loud voice.

We turned, as a breathless constable came doubling up.

"A very dangerous criminal," O'Shea replied, "and we were chasing him. Quick, officer! on which side of the Bridge shall we find a boat?"

The manner of one accustomed to give orders is unmistakable, and:

"West, sir," the constable answered promptly. "There's a boat at the pier."

"Good," said O'Shea, and started to run to the car. I followed.

As we jumped in, turned, and headed back to where Big Ben recorded the fact that only seven minutes had elapsed since we had passed St. James's Palace, I saw the constable coming after us. But, leaving the car by the foot of the clock tower, O'Shea raced across to the gate at the head of those steps that lead down to the pier. It was locked; and here I thought that the chase ended. But I had counted without O'Shea.

London, unlike New York, normally is a very empty city at two o'clock in the morning; but now, as if conjured up by a magic talisman, a group began to assemble. I looked to my right—from which the constable was bearing down upon us. Even as he ran, his bearing was ominous. It occurred to me that he regarded O'Shea and myself with justifiable suspicion, and I foresaw complications.

It was odd, I reflected, that we stood almost in the shadow of Scotland Yard—representing Law and Order, the forces of Empire against those of disruption—but that the very powers that should have backed us were likely now to aid and abet a dangerous conspirator and assassin in escaping the meshes of justice.

The constable rather windily began to blow his whistle again.

A resolute-looking man, clean-shaven, and of a very hard-bitten countenance, suddenly appeared at my elbow.

"What's the trouble?" he inquired—and challenged me with keen eyes.

An official note in his voice was recognizable. O'Shea turned quickly. The ever-increasing group drew more closely around us. A second constable was making his way across from Parliament Square.

"The trouble is," said O'Shea, "that this gate is locked, and I want to get on to the pier."

The man, whose face seemed to have been chiselled out of seasoned teak, stared in a curious way. Then the breathless constable burst upon us.

"Just a minute!" he began. "I want to know some more about this business!"

He became uneasily aware of the presence of our weatherbeaten acquaintance. He stopped in the act of laying his hand upon O'Shea's arm. O'Shea, watching the man who had accosted us, spoke, and:

"Sergeant Donoghue!" he said.

The expression on the grim face changed. The man so addressed drew himself smartly to attention. It was automatic—second nature; but his smile was good to see.

"Thank you, sir," said he, "for remembering me."

O'Shea held out his hand.

"Stand easy, Sergeant," he replied. "I gather that you have left the Army and rejoined the Police."

Donoghue's eyes were glistening as he grasped the proffered hand.

"I have that, sir," he said, "and without loss of rank. I am a detective-sergeant now."

He glanced at the two constables—for the Parliament Square reinforcement had come up.

"Carry on," he directed, "there's a man drowning. Leave this to me."

"Donoghue," said O'Shea, "do you hate the Reds?"

"I do, sir!"

"Well, one of them has just jumped off the Bridge. He is a powerful swimmer. I want to get on to the pier and into a boat."

"You are in luck, sir," Donoghue returned enthusiastically, "for to-night I happen to have the key."

When, a minute later, we pushed out into the stream, watched by an ever-increasing group of idlers, I thought how proud a man must feel to see a light like that which had crossed Donoghue's face as he had recognized the officer he had served under. One such silent tribute is worth more than a thousand cheers.

"Do you remember the night behind the farm, sir?" Donoghue asked.

And O'Shea in reply merely laid his hand upon his shoulder and gripped hard for a moment. But this apparently simple question had a far-reaching result, as I was presently to learn.

A fairly strong current was running, which, together with O'Shea's recollection of the swimmer's position as seen from the Bridge, sufficiently indicated where we should lay our course.

Certain official steps had automatically been taken, and we were not alone in our quest. Apparently, even at two o'clock in the morning, it is contrary to County Council regulations for anyone to bathe from Westminster Bridge.

Looking up from that unfamiliar viewpoint at certain London landmarks outlined against the clear sky, I wondered why Fate always seems to put a brake upon our joy-rides.

Untrammelled by an intense anxiety on account of Nanette that obsessed me to-night, this queer adventure must have been definitely enjoyable. But, like so many human experiences, it was less exciting in the doing than it is in the telling. For exploration of unfamiliar by-paths, as I have already mentioned, there is no vehicle like a cosy armchair.

That Zara would head for the nearest landing place, it was fairly reasonable to suppose. Therefore we pulled hard across in the direction of the County Hall, eagerly watching the surface of the water. Suddenly:

"There he goes!" cried Donoghue.

But, even as he spoke, I had seen the swimmer—close in, under the right bank, heading powerfully for the stairs. We raced for him and made land almost simultaneously.

In the act of landing Zara stumbled and slipped back into the river.

He came up by the stern of the boat. O'Shea's hand shot out, grasped him by a soddened collar-band, and hauled him in against the side. Dimly, I could see O'Shea's face as he looked down at the upcast eyes of Zara. I think I knew what was in his mind, and in those upturned eyes was recognition of it—and acceptance.

Still grasping the helpless man, O'Shea glanced quickly at Donoghue.

"Yes, Donoghue," he said coldly, "I remember the night behind the farm. You have reminded me that I once had decent instincts. Sergeant, here's your prisoner."

CHAPTER XXXI
HIATUS

I FIND THAT MY memory holds no proper record of the hour that elapsed between this time and our return to Nanette. There were certain unavoidable formalities to be gone through; but within ten minutes of the arrest of Zara, I was on the telephone to my rooms. My man answered; and his replies, whilst reticent, were reassuring.

"Mr. Milton has been removed to hospital, sir. A very narrow escape, I understand. It will be a long job, but he is in no danger. Yes, sir, the lady is"—pause—"still here."

"Why?" I asked uneasily, and glanced at O'Shea, who was standing at my elbow throughout this conversation.

"They—didn't like to move her, sir. I 'phoned to Sir Frank Leslie, in Harley Street, sir, by request. He is here."

"But where is—the lady?"

"Sorry, sir, but she is—in your room. Her mother is with her, sir."

"Is she dangerously ill?"

"I don't really know, sir. Both the medical men are with her now."

As I replaced the receiver, I stared at O'Shea. He had moved away from me and was pacing restlessly up and down the bleakly furnished room in New Scotland Yard from which we had been speaking.

"You understand?" I said. "She is—rather badly hurt."

"I understand." He nodded grimly. "She saved my life, Decies, perhaps at the price of her own. I can't bear to think of it."

He turned abruptly and stared out of the window at a vista of empty Embankment below, lighted by many twinkling lamps.

"I have been a self-reliant man all my life, Decies; it may be aggressively so. Perhaps this is poetic justice. Since the moment that I set foot in Madeira, up to this very hour, she has done my work for me, step by step. You admit it, Decies? You admit it?"

"I do," said I. "It's true, but no discredit to you."

He shook his head and resumed the restless pacing. I saw him groping for his monocle, which he had left at his rooms prior to setting out for the raid on the S Group, and I saw him snap his fingers irritably as he realized how enslaved he was to this habit.

"I have placed independence above every other virtue in man," he went on. "I have fought for it and suffered for it. I suppose she has been sent to teach me that independence and loneliness are inseparable. Do you know," he turned and looked fully into my eyes, with an expression almost of humility, "I don't think I could bear that lonely path any longer, Decies. And if—" he paused and squared his jaw for a moment—"and if I have to follow it, there won't be very much left."

"Shut up!" I said. "You are talking nonsense. If you elect to be lonely in future, the choice is yours."

"Unless..." he smiled wryly.

"Don't think of that!" I replied. "She is young and full of stamina. Besides, she wants to live."

"And I want her to live," he added softly. "Yet, even now, I can't believe it—and I can't quite condone it."

"Condone what?" I demanded.

"The acceptance, by a man of my age, world-worn, a little disappointed, more than a little cynical, of such a sacrifice, from a girl with all the world to choose from. I can find no justification."

"I see," I murmured. "And can you find any for leaving her, now that you know? Because you can't shut your eyes to the fact that this is not a schoolgirl's infatuation, but the real thing. Can you condone that?"

My voice was not quite steady.

"She was ready to die for you, O'Shea," I said. "It would break her heart to lose you. Damn it!" I pulled out my cigarette case, "I am talking like your sentimental aunt."

O'Shea smiled, this time more happily, and grasped my shoulder in characteristic fashion.

"I believe we are both behaving rather idiotically," he admitted. "Let's hope for the best."

"I don't believe you would recognize it if it came to you," I returned.

He shrugged his shoulders and we went up to a room on the floor above, where some sort of superior official was waiting. Throughout the interview that followed O'Shea became again the steely-eyed, square-jawed soldier whom I knew so well; the traditional O'Shea, whose name had been a tonic to many a man during those black days when the shadow of Prussia lay over Europe.

CHAPTER XXXII
THE HEART OF NANETTE

I SEEMED TO DETECT an ominous air of hush as I opened the door for O'Shea and myself to go up to my apartments. Nanette's mother met us. I could scarcely bear to look at her. Almost immediately, she fixed her eyes upon O'Shea.

"Major O'Shea," she began bravely, "I have known for a long time how Nanette felt about you...."

"And I suppose you have reproached me," said he.

"I have not," she returned. "I have had many opportunities of watching, and I know that your behaviour has been admirable, if..." she hesitated.

"Yes?" O'Shea urged gently.

"If she has really meant anything to you. Be frank with me, Major O'Shea. Has she?"

"She has," he replied gravely. "I didn't know, but I know now."

"It is frightfully hard to say," she went on, "but..." she turned to me impulsively. "Can you help me, Mr. Decies?"

"I think I can," said I. "There is no reason why my friend, Major O'Shea, should not marry Nanette, unless there is any on your side. Personally, he thinks he is too old for her!" This last remark I added in what was meant to be a facetious manner, for the situation was difficult to cope with. "But please tell us—how is she?"

"She will recover," was the reply, "thanks to the speedy attention that she received. Failing this, it might have been—otherwise. I am afraid she cannot be moved for some time, Mr. Decies. It will be a dreadful inconvenience for you...."

"And a great honour," I added. "Is it possible to see her?"

"I don't know if it is advisable. But she is asking to see"—glancing at O'Shea—"someone."

O'Shea bit his lip—the nearest approach to a display of emotion that I had ever observed in him—and turned quickly aside.

Then followed a period of waiting. Nanette's girl friend came down, having been relieved by a professional nurse. She smiled at O'Shea, and blushed furiously; an unusual accomplishment in a girl of her type and age. But the smile and the blush told me more of the state of Nanette's heart than a long dissertation could have revealed.

The young medical officer appeared at last, and his expression was reassuring.

"Can we go up?" I asked.

"Yes," he replied; "I have Sir Frank's permission to admit you for three minutes, but no more than three minutes."

He stared significantly at O'Shea.

In a queerly furtive fashion I began to mount the stairs of my own house, treading softly as upon holy ground and going with bated breath. O'Shea moved equally silently. I cannot say what his feelings were at this moment, for I did not even look at him. But when we came to the door of the sick room that had been my bedroom, it was opened by a white-capped nurse, and we entered, catlike as burglars.

Nanette lay propped up in my bed, with closed eyes. She was pale, but, in that hour, more adorable than ever. Her mother sat over by an open window, watching, and Sir Frank Leslie stood beside the bed. We crept forward, abashed as detected criminals. But Nanette did not stir, until:

"Someone has come to say good-night to you, dear," said her mother.

Then the drooping lids quivered, and she raised her blue eyes. I cannot say if she saw O'Shea, or merely pretended that she did not see him; but admittedly he was standing behind me. She laid her hand in mine, and:

"Thank you, Mr. Decies," she murmured, in a pathetically weak voice. "I am going to be a frightful nuisance to you. In future, I shall try to arrange to be shot in my own bedroom."

She closed her eyes again, wearily, and dropped her hand upon the coverlet. Sir Frank beckoned to me to step aside. I did so.

O'Shea drew nearer.

"I have come to thank you, Nanette," he said.

He sat on the chair beside her, bending forward. Slowly, she turned her head, raised weary lids again, and looked at him. She stayed so for what seemed a very long time; just looking—looking—and questioning. He stooped nearer and nearer, until suddenly, but very weakly, a white arm crept around his neck and little trembling fingers were plunged into his hair.

Nanette drew his head down upon the pillow beside her, sighed, and closed her eyes again happily.

I turned away, staring at her mother. Then I caught Sir Frank's glance. He began to tiptoe toward the door, nodded significantly to the nurse—and shepherded us out of the sick room!

The last to leave, I looked back, guiltily, for one moment. Nanette was fast asleep, for they had given her an opiate. And she lay with her head nestling upon O'Shea's shoulder.

I shall always remember her smile.